NO LIMITS. NO RULES.

"Get your coat, we have to find Flower." Proctor stood for a moment, watching the rain. "We'll start with the cabins. There's what, six? Eight? Then the main building. There has to be a cellar or an attic—we were too quick before, and we missed it somehow."

They stepped outside; the rain was light and steady.

Taz snapped up his collar, snapped his fingers once, and seemed to make up his mind. "No rules?"

Proctor nodded. "No rules."

They started with the first cabin and found nothing until they reached the last one.

Like the others, the door was locked and they battered it open.

Proctor went first, stopped, and barely heard Taz moan at his shoulder, "Oh God."

The stench of blood was nearly overwhelming. . . .

BLACK OAK 1

GENESIS

by

Charles Grant

A ROC BOOK

ROC
Published by the Penguin Group
Penguin Putnam Inc., 375 Hudson Street,
New York, New York 10014, U.S.A.
Penguin Books Ltd, 27 Wrights Lane,
London W8 5TZ, England
Penguin Books Australia Ltd, Ringwood,
Victoria, Australia
Penguin Books Canada Ltd, 10 Alcorn Avenue,
Toronto, Ontario, Canada M4V 3B2
Penguin Books (N.Z.) Ltd, 182–190 Wairau Road,
Auckland 10, New Zealand

Penguin Books Ltd, Registered Offices:
Harmondsworth, Middlesex, England

First published by Roc, an imprint of Dutton NAL,
a member of Penguin Putnam Inc.

First Printing, May, 1998
10 9 8 7 6 5 4 3 2

 REGISTERED TRADEMARK—MARCA REGISTRADA

Printed in the United States of America

This is for Bill, USPS, without whose patience
and lousy jokes I'd have a whole lot
of manuscripts in my house;

And Barbara, USPS, the same but
a lot cuter. Except for the jokes.

Thank you both.

ONE

The sky was still light, no stars yet, no moon. But the river-split valley was already dark, the Cumberland Mountains hiding the last of the sun. Bands of thick mist reached out of the woods, curling under at the road, like claws ready to pull a great beast from the trees.

The headlights only made it worse, making the black more dark, and the trees that crowded the verge more like a solid wall.

Sloan Delany rubbed his eyes with the knuckles of his left hand and reluctantly decided it might be time to give it up and change direction.

On the other hand, surrendering now would mean ending his vacation without reaching the final goal.

Unlike others he knew, who either headed for resorts or stayed home to mow the lawn, he went on the road and searched for places that sold the worst kitsch he could find. A shop in Pennsylvania, where he picked up tiny Amish farmers carved out of potatoes and lacquered; a roadside stand outside Ottawa where he found, of all things, a matching pair of varnished piranha mounted on coral stands; a store in Memphis, with Elvis in loincloth salt and pepper shakers.

Sometimes he flew to a city like Salt Lake, or Chicago . . . rented a car and drove. It didn't make any difference, as long as he found something that would add bizarre class to his collection and, in the bargain, make his friends wince and wonder about his mind.

Roadside America was his cultural Bible; off-kilter museums his shrines.

This time it was a place someone had told him about while he'd been in Lexington, trying to decide whether the crocheted Secretariat toilet covers were neat, or just tasteless. He had strict unwritten tests based primarily on instinct, and the covers, eventually, did not pass.

The new information, however, was intriguing. The bartender had no map, just vague directions to an area called Crockston in the eastern part of the state, and he had figured he could check it out on the way home.

Assuming, that is, that he could find the damn place.

One pickup heading in the opposite direction had been the only other vehicle he had seen in the past hour. There were two well-kept campgrounds, but the offices had been empty; a collection of houses in a clearing that grazed the road had darkened windows, although the dogs when he approached them made enough racket to raise the dead.

The mist shattered against the windshield.

The road climbed and fell in slow curves.

He rubbed his eyes again, and yawned so widely his jaw popped.

Every so often something glittered in the trees, specks of different colors. Animal eyes. Shards of glass. Mica in the occasional moss-draped boulder.

The radio produced nothing but static, or rapid tinny voices too faint to understand.

Finally he opened the window a little, just for the wind-noise, just for the sound.

This, he thought, is stupid. Go home, boy, go home, forget it.

Another mile, and he realized the sky had finally gone dark, and a pale moon sat over the mountains. Its feeble light helped some, but not enough. The trees were still too dark, the road still too empty.

Maybe he should just give it up. Find the next major intersection and head east into Virginia. If he were lucky, he'd come on the interstate fairly soon, which would mean a motel and a restaurant. And people. If he got up early and pushed it, he could be home by midnight tomorrow. It wasn't as if he didn't have enough stuff in his trunk—pieces for his collection, and some gifts for the guys, who would tell him he was nuts and that he ought to save his money.

All except Proctor.

Proctor knew.

Proctor understood.

Delany wasn't about to save his money, because there was nothing, or anyone, to save it for, and he sure as hell wasn't going to take what little there was in the bank with him.

Proctor knew; he understood.

A speed-limit sign glared past, pocked with rusted bullet holes.

"For God's sake," he muttered, "don't these people need directions? What, are they all goddamn Daniel Boone?"

The magic words.

On the left side of a sharp eastward curve, almost hidden by trailing branches, he saw the billboard: *Cumberland Motel and Museum of the Odd. 5 miles*

"Bingo," he shouted, and slapped the steering wheel with his palms. "About goddamn time."

He crossed a bridge with open-girder sides, saw black water carrying sparkling highlights of the moon; he followed another curve into a long tunnel that had no lights at all, and no sign it would ever end.

You're tired, boy, he told himself; thinking like that's gonna spook you into a bottle.

Still, he was relieved to see the moon on the other side, and wished he could see some animals on the road, dead or alive. So far there had been nothing, not even a bird.

He hummed the *Twilight Zone* theme, glanced at the empty passenger seat, and said, "You want to see something really scary?"

He laughed, and raised a triumphant fist when he spotted the light up ahead, on the right. A glaring white flood that slowed the car and let him breathe easily.

His destination was a long log cabin with a deep porch and a high slanted roof, a crushed-gravel parking lot to its right, and what looked to be smaller cabins ranged north on the left. A smaller sign at the entrance matched the billboard's plain lettering; a neon sign just below it promised him a vacancy. If there was peeling paint or sagging beams, holes in the roof or weeds, the darkness hid them.

He pulled in beside the main building, switched off the ignition, and closed his eyes for a moment. This time the silence was gentle, not a threat. He blew out, shook himself, and opened the door.

"Damn!"

It was Wednesday in mid-October, but the mountain air was winter-chilled, catching him by surprise. A hard hand rubbed across his face; he reached into the backseat and grabbed his suitcase, stamped the ground a little to bring his legs back to life, and headed for the porch.

Ignoring the mist his shoes kicked into tatters.

Inside, the place felt fireplace warm.

On the left was a large room, long tables set for family-style dining, each table with matching long benches; on the right a gift shop that didn't look too promising—standard display cases with standard Appalachian items arranged on white cloth. Bare hardwood floors; framed oils and watercolors on the walls, all for sale. Local artists, he reckoned by all the hand-lettered signs, and by the looks of them, not all that good.

Neither room was occupied, not even a waitress or clerk trying to look busy.

Directly ahead was a paneled registration desk framed by gleaming dark wood; no one there either.

He raised an eyebrow, called a "Hello?" and startled himself at how loud he sounded.

He was startled a second time when he heard a muffled response, and had nearly completed a full turn looking for the source, when a door opened behind the counter and a woman stepped out. Smiling. Wiping her hands on a towel.

"Sorry," she said as he walked over. "Didn't hear you over the TV."

He could hear it now, the clear sound of a baseball game.

She didn't seem to be much younger than he, probably in her late forties. Brown hair cropped pragmatically short, lean and lightly tanned, in a plaid shirt with rolled-up sleeves, and jeans that hung slightly loose.

He set the suitcase down and massaged the small of his back with one hand. "Got a room?"

"Cabins."

"No problem." Another look at the dining room. "Am I the only one tonight?"

She slid a short form in front of him, dropped a ballpoint beside it. "Nope. Couple of hunters. They're already racked for the night."

As he filled in the information he asked about the chances of getting something to eat, and was told the kitchen was open most of the day. A grin: "That is, when I'm around and awake."

He returned the grin, and after completing the registration, asked about the museum's hours. The look she gave him made him wonder if he'd inadvertently tripped over some local social taboo.

"You're not a reporter," she said, less asking than accusing.

"No. It's what I do on my vacation—look for weird

stuff. Buy really tacky stuff." He gestured vaguely at the gift shop. "Unfortunately, that looks too good for my taste."

Clearly she didn't know whether to laugh or be insulted, not even when he smiled to prove he'd meant no offense and was telling the truth. He held up a finger—*hold on a minute*—and knelt to open his suitcase. He could sense her leaning over the counter as he rummaged through his clothes, feeling his way toward something he'd picked up outside Louisville two days ago.

"Ah." He straightened, and set a pink tissue-paper bundle on the counter between them. "Just to give you an idea."

She stared at it.

"Go ahead, open it, I don't mind."

Still dubious, but finally willing, she took the paper off carefully, blinked, and said, "You have got to be kidding."

It was a glossy ceramic statuette of a Tennessee walker, about five inches high, including the base that was supposed to be a field of grass and looked like two saws with green, rotting teeth. In front of the horse was a tiny black man in a jockey's outfit. Set into the horse's belly was a thermometer.

"You paid money for this?"

"Awful, ain't it," he said proudly.

She nodded, looked at him sideways, touched the top of the horse's head, and nodded again. "You got more of this stuff."

"Right."

"Just as awful."

"Absolutely."

"And at home? On . . . on the mantel?"

"Lord, no. I got a special room." A quick shrug. "Most of it, anyway."

Her smile was broad. It took no years off, but it made him realize she wasn't plain at all. "You unpack, Mr. Delaney—"

"Sloan."

"Sloan." She held out her hand. "Maggie. Maggie Medford. You unpack, freshen up, I'll have some dinner waiting for you in an hour. Nothing fancy." Another look at the walker. "Better than that, though, I hope. Then I'll show you the museum."

He almost agreed, but was interrupted by a yawn that seemed to go on forever. When it was over, his eyes had watered and there was a near cramp in his neck.

"Better idea," he suggested, apologizing with a look. "I have to leave pretty much first thing, and I'm obviously more tired than I thought. Could we . . . I mean, would it be okay if we did the museum now, then eat? If I go back to the room now, I'm not leaving, believe me."

"Your dime," she said, unconcerned.

"My dime."

"Actually," she said, holding out a palm and waggling her fingers, "it's five bucks."

Now this, Delany thought gleefully, is what I live for.

The Museum of the Odd was in a long room behind the gift shop, reached through double glass doors Maggie slid aside from the center, under a flickering neon sign that announced its name.

There was no overhead lighting.

Here, despite the cool of the night outside, the air-conditioning was still on, just enough to feel it across the shoulders, along the arms.

Worn carpeting on the floor muffled his footsteps, and it was too dim to make out the pattern; just a series of dark splotches.

On either side of a center aisle were waist-high display cases lit from within. The oddities they contained were similar to those he had seen before—roots shaped like faces or small animals or human babies in fetal positions; animal skeletons, each with a deformity that ranged from swollen skulls to multiple limbs; a glittering rock, supposedly a meteorite; geodes; a small open book bound in cracked hide, allegedly a diary belonging to Daniel Boone; a yellowed scrap of paper the 3x5 card beside it claimed held Andrew Jackson's signature; a page from another book, claiming an eighteenth century prophecy of both World Wars.

A tangle of moss said to be the Devil's hair.

Maggie followed him, saying nothing as he examined each one, grunting his pleasure, shaking his head only once—at the Devil's hair—and looking at her with a half smile, receiving only a shrug in return.

The air smelled of cinnamon and warm wood.

There were questions he wanted to ask, but speaking in this quiet place seemed curiously sacrilegious. What he wanted to know would have to wait.

He took his time, saving what he hoped was the best, for last.

In the rear wall was a niche, which held a glass

cylinder some seven feet high and lit from below. It was filled with liquid, and a constant veil of bubbles large and small drifted slowly upward.

He couldn't read the card taped to its dusty wood base, but he didn't have to.

"Well," he whispered. "Well."

Maggie stood close behind him, and he could almost feel her lips when she whispered in his ear, "It killed my husband, you know.

TWO

The trio sat at the square dining-room table, staring at a photograph lying in the table's center. A brass hanging lamp with a dark green shade had been pulled down so far, little of its glow reached beyond them.

The rest of the room was either shapes or shadows, save where the glow was reflected in a picture window in the back wall. There, there were three ghosts.

And outside was the wind.

"He's kidding, right?" A young man, with long thick hair that drifted in waves to his shoulders. Large dark eyes with extravagant lashes, high cheeks, and smooth skin made him look even younger. He wore a black T-shirt and jeans, his bare feet hooked over the front rung of his chair. "I mean, he's got to be kidding."

The woman who sat opposite him made a face but said nothing beyond a grunt that meant nothing. She had straight black hair that didn't quite reach her shoulders, and straight black bangs that covered her brow. Curious looks. He couldn't decide if she was Mexican or something else. Not that it mattered; she was twenty years older than he at least, and treated him like a baby brother.

"Well? He's kidding, right?"

On his left was a lean man in a dark grey tailored suit, maroon club tie with matching handkerchief set perfectly in the jacket pocket. Bald, hook nose, eyes too deeply set to catch the light. "I wouldn't know."

Paul Tazaretti raked a hand through his hair. "I still don't get it. What does Mr. Proctor want me to do?"

The woman held up one finger—*pay attention, Taz.* "Gently, oval head." She pointed at the photograph.

"Okay."

"Large eyes completely black, almost a teardrop shape. All in all, a classic design."

"Yeah. So?"

She pointed again. "A very thin torso, smooth, unable to tell the sex. The skin is dull white, maybe light grey."

Taz rolled his eyes. "I can see that, Lana. Jeez." He turned to the older man. "Come on, Doc, gimme a break here, huh? This is too weird."

"Nothing weird about it, Paul," Doc answered calmly, his hands folded loosely on the table. Only Doc ever called him Paul. A forefinger poked out toward the photograph. "It is, considering the time of day, a perfectly clear, adequately composed, fairly well-lighted photograph. I do not see what you are so upset about."

Before Taz could answer, Lana said, "Look again."

He sighed to let them know how put-upon he was, then picked up a small magnifying glass and held it over the photograph. "All right, all right." He examined the distorted image as best he could. "So he looks like he's making his way toward those trees in the back. He was looking back where he came from when whoever it was took the picture."

Doc grunted.

Taz grunted as well, mocking him, but leaned closer, shifting the glass around the photograph. Slowly. Again. When he recentered on the figure he leaned closer still. As far as he could tell, there were no matte lines or false shadows to indicate that the figure had been superimposed on this field, or pasture, or wherever the hell it was.

He looked up at Lana. "At least I don't see any zippers on his back."

She grinned, and pushed a finger across her straight black bangs, nudging them away from her eyes. "*Invaders from Mars.*"

He winked.

She said, "Don't be so smug, Taz. It doesn't prove a thing."

Tell me about it, he thought sourly. But they really can't believe this stupid thing is real.

"About five feet tall," he estimated, turning the photograph slightly, tilting his head as he did.

"Really," said Doc. "How do you figure that?"

"That fence on the left. He's not far from it, and not much taller than the top rail. It's hard to tell from the angle, but I'd say about five feet."

The wind was nearly silent, but not silent enough, whispering just at the fringe of his hearing. It gave him the creeps, sitting here in the near dark.

The picture gave him the creeps too. He didn't know why, exactly; maybe it was the look on the creature's face—fear at having been caught, terror at seeing what had caught him. Maybe it was the fact that the people he worked for seldom dismissed such things out of hand.

The funny thing was, even at the beginning, two years ago, he hadn't thought they were nuts.

He should have, but he hadn't.

Lana shifted impatiently, and Doc coughed softly into a fist.

Finally he dropped the glass and sat back. "I don't know what else to tell you, except that it's a fake."

"And what," said Doc calmly, "makes you reach that conclusion."

"Because it is," he insisted.

"That's no answer, Paul."

Taz had had enough. He nearly rose as high as his voice: "Look at it!"

"I am looking, Paul."

"The damn thing's got fangs, Doc!" He dropped back into his chair, nearly panting. "The son of a bitch is a space vampire!"

No one said a word.

The house was silent save for an occasional creak when a gust of wind pushed at the walls.

I've blown it, he thought miserably; damn, I've blown it.

Then Doc leaned back, his face pulling out of the light. Except for thin lips pulled back in a smile.

Lana swallowed. And finally giggled.

Taz opened his mouth. "You . . ." He closed it, and blushed when Lana's giggles became a laugh she tried to wave away with apologetic fingers. "Oh, funny," he snarled, and reached for the photograph. "Really funny." He flipped it over, flipped it back, and shook his head in disgust. "This is one of Delany's, right? It's got to be one of his. Who else would want something this dumb."

The picture window shimmered when the wind slid across it, and the ghosts seemed to ripple.

Doc half rose from his seat, hooked a finger in the ring at the lamp's base, and pushed it up; the light spread. He reached behind him then to flick a switch, and the room expanded, the shadows became furniture—the table, a breakfront, a serving table beside a doorway that led into the small kitchen.

"Ha," Taz said. "Ha and ha." He stood, brushed a hand down his chest, and added, "Ha."

"Now, Taz," the woman chided softly.

"Yeah, yeah, I know." He walked around the table, paused behind her for a moment as if he would touch her hair, then stepped through the wide archway into the living room. A three-cushion couch had its back to him, flanked by a pair of slightly battered end tables, and fronted by a long walnut coffee table on which was a neat pile of manila folders, and a telephone with a built-in answering machine. To his left was an open hallway that led to four other rooms; to his right another hall, closed off by a heavy oak door.

No one but Proctor went through there without specific invitation.

Most of the left-hand wall was taken up by a ceiling-high, glass-door bookcase whose panes were lightly etched with roses and grapevines. Directly ahead was a window half again as long as the one at his back, this one overlooking the Hudson River from the top of the Palisades; on its right was a door that led to a narrow redwood deck. On the right-hand wall was another bookcase, this one used for the TV, the VCR, the stereo system, and dozens of tapes and compact discs, magazines and folders. Two armchairs faced the sofa at angles left and right; a third, a wingback, sat between the coffee table and the window.

Although the room was large, the ceiling high, what little it contained didn't seem lost. Mismatched and well used, it was comfortable; a place to relax in as well as work.

It ought to be; it was Proctor's home.

He flipped over the sofa's back, landed with an insulted "humph!", and stretched out, hands behind his head, head on one armrest, heels on the other.

"You think I fell for it, don't you," he said, staring angrily at the ceiling.

He heard chairs sliding back across the carpet.

"Of course you did," Doc said, not unkindly. "You—"

Taz waved a hand. "I know, I know, I didn't take it all in. I didn't consider all the facts."

"Including . . .?"

He mumbled something.

"Sorry?" Doc said.

"The source," he admitted. "Okay? I didn't ask for and then evaluate the source before I . . . oh, hell." Using the rounded back as a grip, he pulled himself up, rested his chin on his folded hands. "Delany's?"

Lana nodded. "It came Saturday. He got it in Kentucky, at the Barlow Creek Space Repository."

He grinned. "The what?"

"The Barlow Creek Space Repository. Apparently the owner spends his vacations in spaceships." A pause. "He says he's their tour guide."

"Well, hey, whatever turns him on." He let himself slip onto his back again, sighing when Doc came around the sofa and slapped his feet off the armrest. "Sorry."

"Don't be sorry," Doc said, taking the chair on the left. "Just don't do it."

Taz swung his feet to the floor and sat up. Doc spooked him when he acted like this. He'd rather the man yell, which is what he usually did. Then he wasn't so unnerving.

"Now," Doc said. He picked up a folder and opened it in his lap. A glance at his watch, but no visible reaction. "You're sure about this?"

Taz nodded. "He makes out tow tickets every time he talks the customer into paying cash. He gives one to the customer, who pays. He gives the other to the boss, showing a smaller amount, and pockets the difference." He rubbed the side of his head vigorously. "As near as I can see, he does it maybe five or six times a month. He's not outrageous with the prices and stuff, and doesn't seem to be greedy, so no one complains. The customers, I mean."

Doc nodded. "So he's taking away . . . what?"

"Four, five hundred a month that I can be sure of." The older man frowned.

Taz shifted. "That's not out of line, Doc. A busy place like that, you've got cars and trucks coming in all the time. It also does school buses for a couple of towns. Fender work, door work, stuff inside, upholstery and stuff like that. . . ." He shrugged. "The guy's the super. He's been there just about eight years, so the boss, Lozario, doesn't watch him. Doesn't watch anyone else, for that matter, that I can see. I took a ton of breaks, and nobody seemed to care as long as I did the work."

"If you say so, Paul."

Taz looked at him steadily. "I say so, Doc."

Doc closed the folder with a snap. "Then I think Mr. Proctor will be very pleased."

Taz resisted the temptation to preen. This hadn't been his first case, but it was the first without direct supervision. He didn't know if they had deliberately given him an easy one or not, and he didn't care.

What mattered was, he had pulled it off without suspicion.

Doc checked his watch again. "Nine." Two fingers adjusted his pocket handkerchief. "I do not think he's coming soon. Lana?"

She poked her head out of the kitchen.

Doc tapped his watch face and shook his head.

She shrugged. "Okay. I'm kind of tired anyway."

Taz didn't know exactly how to react. He was, on the one hand, pleased he would be able to get home early. Yet he had hoped to have spent some time with Proctor. The man was strange, no question about it. But he knew so much damn weird stuff, Taz didn't think he'd ever get to learn half of it.

Doc rose stiffly and massaged the back of his neck. "I'll lock up."

Taz glanced at the locked door that led to the other wing as he slipped his feet into his trainers. "Are you sure he's not coming?"

Doc didn't bother to answer.

The air was damp, and Taz rolled his shoulders against a faint chill. The back of the house faced the road, but no one could see it—a dense row of tall evergreens lined the three-acre property from one end to the other, then marched down the sides to the edge of the Palisades cliff. Not even the closest neighbors could see through the heavy boughs.

They stood on the back porch, the only light a small yellow bulb over the lintel. A moth slapped against it repeatedly, barely audible.

Lana held the neck of her light sweater closed, gave a quick wave and hurried down the steps. The driveway was at the end of a short brick walk, her sedan last in line. A flash of her headlights a moment later, and she backed out into the street, flashed the lights at them again and was gone.

Taz was next, but he didn't want to go.

He slipped his hands into his jeans pockets, thumbs out, and hunched his shoulders. Stalling. Glancing over his shoulder at the moth, and the yellow bulb that was supposed to repel it.

"It's all right," Doc told him quietly, taking his elbow and leading him down the steps. "I understand." At Taz's more rust than metal Jeep, he added, "It rather takes the wind from your sails. Him not being here, that is."

He nodded. "Yeah. I was, you know, hoping." He squinted over the hood, at the way the long ranch stretched into the dark. One man, or an army, could be out there, and he wouldn't know it. "Oh, well, no big deal."

Doc grunted; it might have been a laugh, but it definitely called him a liar.

Taz grinned. After two years working for Black Oak Security, he should be used to it by now. He wasn't. He didn't think he ever would be. The office is in a house, not some bigass building in the city across the river; they meet mostly in the evening because their investigative work takes up their days; and when they do meet, half the time the talk's about the weirdest damn stuff, the kind of off-the-wall stuff he liked to watch on TV or in the movies—vampires, space guys, people who talk to the dead, people who talk to people who don't exist, ghosts.

If it wasn't for the money he needed, he'd be hard-pressed to explain why he stayed around.

Liar.

He scratched behind one ear. "Doc, what about that Blaine guy?"

"What about him, Paul?"

"Well, he keeps calling. Don't you think you should have talked to him?"

Doc adjusted his topcoat's collar. "That's not our job."

"Yeah, but—"

"No buts. Mr. Proctor will talk to him if he wishes. You know the system. You know how it works. The message will be passed on. That's all we can do." Doc touched Taz's arm with a stiff finger. A warning. "That's all we're supposed to do."

Yeah, maybe, he thought, but it's a hell of a way to run a business.

"Paul. As much as I enjoy the company, truly, I really have no intention of spending the night in this driveway. I have a long day in the city tomorrow, and I need my rest." Doc nudged him until he slid in behind the wheel. "Tomorrow's Thursday. End the job Friday morning. Make it loud, so Mr. Lozario can fire you, as arranged, then come around for lunch on Monday. Late. Mr. Proctor will want to hear all the gory details.''

He smiled briefly, slapped Taz's shoulder, and walked away.

Taz backed into the street, grimaced when the gears refused to mesh cleanly, and sped away, heading south toward Fort Lee.

Gory details.

He laughed aloud.

Only Doc would think the exposure of a simple scam—even one that had probably cost Lozario over thirty, forty grand—would have gory details.

Weird, he thought; I got some weird people here.

It wasn't until he was halfway home that he realized they'd forgotten to turn on the answering machine.

Within seconds after Doc Falcon's car left, the neighborhood was silent.

Except for the wind as it passed through the trees, softly hissing.

Except for the moth battering itself to death against the yellow bulb.

Except for the muffled sound of a telephone ringing inside.

THREE

. . . it killed my husband.

Delany bit down on the inside of his cheek, trusting the sharp pain to keep him from snickering. Or from jumping when the woman laid a palm on his back and eased around to stand beside him.

"Killed him, you say," he said evenly, nodding politely.

"Oh, yes." Still whispering.

Delany, m'boy, he thought, this had better be a damn good story, or you've got a nut here and you'll have to lock the doors and windows.

He glanced at her sideways, watching as her left hand reached up to the cylinder and trailed fingertips down the smooth glass.

Slowly.

Almost caressingly.

"Oh . . . yes."

Her hip brushed against him as she reached out again, rising up on her toes, not quite able to reach the top. She looked at him with a one-sided smile. Mocking or seductive, he couldn't say.

It didn't matter; he didn't like it.

The dim light gave her face planes and angles in

the wrong places, and the bubbles that rose lazily from bottom to top rippled shadows across it. Her lips were too dark; her skin much too pale.

"Forgive me for saying so," he said, watching those fingers move, "but you don't sound too broken up about it."

"A long time ago, Mr. Delany. A long time ago."

"Sloan."

She nodded, just once.

He touched the cylinder himself, and shuddered.

It was cold.

Her fingers wrapped over his hand and gently eased it away. "It's fragile, Sloan," she told him. "I'd rather you didn't."

Her fingers left him, and he couldn't help it—he rubbed the skin slowly, until it warmed up.

He cleared his throat softly, and said, "If it's not too much my asking, what happened?"

"You know," she said, staring at the exhibit, tilting her head slightly, and ignoring the question, "you're the first one to come here in a very long time."

He followed a bubble to the top before saying, "Well, I'm not an expert on this part of the country, mind you, but you do seem a little out of the way."

"Not that much out of the way. We get our hunters now and then."

"But they don't visit the museum."

"No." She stepped back and crossed her arms over her chest, hands gripping her shoulders. "No, they're not interested in anything but the hunt. Trophies and meat, Sloan. Mostly trophies and meat."

He almost laughed again, wondering what she

thought all this stuff was. What she thought this thing under glass was.

It sure as hell looked like some kind of trophy to him.

The bubbles rose.

The light flickered once, and steadied.

The bubbles rose.

The air-conditioning pushed a draft over his head, and he automatically put a hand there, to smooth the hair back into place.

"Hypnotic, aren't they."

The bubbles rose, big and small.

He tried to find a pattern, some repetitive sequence, to give a hint as to how the aerator worked. Failing that, he began to follow trails up the glass.

"Sometimes I stand here for an hour, just watching."

There were horizontal gaps in the curtain once in a while, and he took to following them. Bottom to top.

Bottom to top.

"It's soothing in a way. It kind of clears my mind."

A single strand of hair slipped over his forehead, tickling as if a tiny insect had landed there. He hooked it back into place with a finger, and that one sharp movement made him realize she was right—the bubbles were hypnotizing. And they prevented him from looking too closely at what they veiled.

He closed his eyes for a moment, tightly, and felt himself begin to sway.

She put a concerned hand on his arm. "Are you all right?"

"Yes," he managed after thinking it over. "A long

ride and no food, my dear. 'Tis a curse of mere mortals."

She laughed silently and took his elbow. "I'm sorry, Sloan, I wasn't thinking." She turned him around. "The kitchen's open, as of now." She led him down the aisle, idly fingerdusting the display cases as they passed. "There isn't much, but you're welcome to what I have."

As she slid the glass doors open, he looked over his shoulder, and could see nothing in the cylinder but a dark shape that seemed to shimmer as the bubbles rose around it.

Good Lord, Proctor, he thought; I've got a good one for you this time.

"How did it happen?"

They sat in the dining room while he worked on an open-face, hot roast beef sandwich with the thickest, best gravy he'd ever had in his life. Mashed potatoes. Beans and lettuce from her garden. Salad. Fresh butter. Warm bread. She refused to let him have coffee while he ate; instead, she poured him a large glass of milk, claiming that the caffeine killed the taste.

She sat across from him, nibbling on buttered bread. And stealing sips from his milk.

It nearly killed him not to wipe off the white mustache on her upper lip.

The way she smiled at him, she knew it too.

"Sorry," he said. "None of my business."

There were three small wagon-wheel chandeliers hanging from the exposed-beam ceiling. Only one was lit.

"No," she said, waving a piece of bread. "It's all right."

While she had been in the kitchen, he'd tried calling Proctor from the registration desk, but no one had answered. It took him a moment to remember it was Wednesday. Proctor might not be back from the nursing home yet. But a call tomorrow. Definitely. This place was too good to pass up.

"I mean," he said around a mouthful of food, "you have to admit it's odd." His smile reached his eyes. "To a stranger like myself, that is. And a Yankee, to boot."

She folded her hands on the bare table and stared at his plate. A slip of brown hair fell over her eyes. He wanted to fix that, too, but didn't dare move. If she was going to tell him, it would be soon, and he didn't want to disrupt whatever debate she was in.

But she would tell.

He knew it.

Proctor claimed it was the Irish so obvious in his face, the way he smiled with every muscle and wrinkle. So friendly that confidence and intimacy were foregone conclusions. Delany had never questioned it; he only knew that his investigations generally produced results.

"I met him in Norfolk," she said softly, not looking up, rubbing one thumb over the other. "I was on vacation, he was on leave. It was back in '84."

"Sailor?"

"Sort of. Pilot. A chopper pilot. He'd put in his twenty and was looking to retire. His daddy left him this place, and he convinced me it would be a good thing to live in the mountains." She lifted her gaze.

"Fresh air, fresh food, nice people dropping by . . . the man had a gift. We were married in three weeks."

He looked around the room. "You seem to be doing all right."

She shrugged. "It pays the bills, I do meet the most fascinating people, and I'm my own boss. I get up when I want to, I do what I have to, and I can leave anytime I want."

He was surprised. "You have help then?"

"Nope. I just shut the place down."

His fork scraped across the plate. He winced and set it down, not realizing how quiet it had grown.

The room shrank then as he felt the empty road at his back, the mountains on all sides, the night. The moon in the windows coating the panes with flat silver.

"There's an airfield," she said. She reached over to pick up his spoon, turned it over in her hands and tapped a palm with the bowl. "About twelve, thirteen miles up the road. Pipers, Cessnas, little planes like that, I never did know what they all were. Anyway, Jack, my husband, he used to go there once a month or so, go up for a few hours, to keep his hand in and his license current." A brief smile, a melancholy lift of a shoulder. "I never went up with him. Those things were too small, scared me half to death."

"Me, too. I want a whole ton of metal around me when I'm flying."

She nodded. "Exactly. You think about it, it's dumb, but he never forced me to go, and never got mad when I didn't."

Tapping the spoon against her palm.

Not making a sound.

"About six years ago he was flying up over Spooner Mountain—that's the one directly behind us—and saw something in a clearing. He never did say what it was, but he couldn't land, so when he got back he got his gear, kissed me, and took off on a hike."

And never came back, Delany thought; I've heard this one a million times.

"I went after him the next afternoon." She made a muscle with her right arm and grinned. "You get healthy around here, hiking and chopping and all that." She put her arm down and began tapping with the spoon again. "It wasn't him staying overnight that bothered me. It happens sometimes. But when he wasn't back for breakfast or lunch, I got worried.

"I reached the clearing just before nightfall.

"I found him."

Wood creaked.

He looked toward the gift shop and frowned. He hadn't remembered when she'd turned out the lights, and all he could see were shapes in there now, grown by dim moonlight.

Wood creaked.

She touched his hand and laughed. "It's the building talking to itself. You get used to it."

Maybe *you* do, he thought.

He picked up his fork, tried another piece of meat, and winced—it was cold, and the gravy had thickened.

"So what did the police say?" he asked, leaning back as he fumbled for his cigarettes.

"I don't know. I didn't tell them."

He used the match and the flame to cover his astonishment. It didn't work, because she was smiling at him, knowing.

"He was torn up, Sloan," she said, looking side to side to avoid looking at his eyes. "I figured it was a bear."

He gestured toward the museum with the cigarette. "That's no bear in there, Maggie."

"I know."

"It looks like—"

"I know."

He watched the tobacco smoke arc away from a draft he couldn't feel; he watched her hands play calmly with the spoon; he watched her watching him with unsettling amusement.

He grinned. "Ah!"

She straightened, and set the spoon back in its place.

"Beautiful innkeeper," he said, using the cigarette to point. "City boy in the country. It's late, he's tired, she has the voice of an angel . . . and the devil's own tongue." He waggled the cigarette like an accusing finger. "Shame on you, Maggie Medford, for telling me tales. And after all I've done for you."

"And what have you done for me?"

"Well, for one thing, I'm not a hunter after trophies and meat."

She laughed and shook her head, reached out and covered his left hand with one of hers. The smile vanished. "And what am I, Mr. Delany, if I'm not a trophy?"

He continued to smile because he couldn't think of anything else to do.

"So I'm beautiful, Mr. Delany?"

He swallowed, but he couldn't force his gaze away from her face, and the expression he saw there.

"Do you want me, Mr. Delany? The lonely widow? Do you want me?"

He tried to move his hand, but her grip was too strong.

She cocked her head. "On this table, or in your bed, Mr. Delany?"

He dropped the cigarette onto his plate and took her wrist, but he couldn't break the grip.

She rose and took his right hand away from hers easily, and pinned it palm down on the table. Leaning heavily on his hands, so close he could smell the kitchen on her, and a faint perfume, and whatever was in her hair, and whatever she used on her lips.

"What?" she whispered huskily. "What do you want, Mr. Delany?"

He pulled; he tugged; he felt his face grow red as the anger rose, at her and at the helplessness. It was stupid. He should be able to free himself with no trouble at all. He had been in scrapes with men twice, three times her size, with barely a bruise to show for it. Yet he couldn't get his goddamn hands loose, and his legs wouldn't let him stand up.

"Sloan," she whispered.

He could feel her breath on his face.

"Sloan?"

He yanked his arms again and nearly slid off the chair and under the table.

Wood creaked.

He let himself sag. "All right, all right. I've obviously offended you, and I'm sorry. Really."

She didn't answer.

"So what do you want, Maggie?"

"What she wants," a voice said, "is an answer to her question."

He jerked his head around, looked down the length of the table, and saw someone there, untouched by the light.

Without warning Maggie released him, and he fell back into his chair. His hands ached, and his lungs wouldn't give him enough air to clear his head.

Until Maggie said, "Don't kill him."

And Delany tried to run.

FOUR

The telephone rang, and no one picked it up.

In a six-room suite high above Park Avenue, an elderly man pushed a meaty hand through thick white hair brushed straight back from his forehead. "Damn. Nine-thirty and still no answer."

"Just as well, Father. Just as well."

Taylor Blaine looked at his son with mild impatience, cradling the receiver none too gently. His dressing gown was old-fashioned—silver-and-burgundy brocade trimmed and belted with black satin. His white shirt was open at the collar, the tie tossed onto the floor beneath the chair. His feet were in stiff-soled slippers; in his right hand he held an unlit cigarette.

"It doesn't make any difference," he said gruffly. "Tonight or tomorrow. I'm still going through with it."

Franklin lifted his hands in a yielding shrug. *I've done my best*, the gesture said; *it's in your hands now.*

"Damn right," Blaine muttered, and glared at the telephone as if it were the cause of all his troubles. A hundred buttons, a hundred little pictographs he couldn't see without his glasses, a hundred messages in tiny print he couldn't see to read even if he had his glasses. In the old days, all you had to do was lift the receiver and bark at the desk clerk or the hotel operator. No computers to contend with; no flashing lights that drove you crazy trying to figure out what they meant.

His children lovingly called him a Luddite; he countered that progress wasn't always what it was cracked up to be.

Especially when all you wanted to do was make a goddamn call.

"You know," he began grumpily.

His son grinned tolerantly. "Yes, Father, I know. In the good old days."

Blaine snarled, then smiled. He was stocky and slightly less than average height, his face a bit more fleshy and lined than the year before, but he figured he was still in pretty good shape for a man three years shy of seventy.

Franklin, on the other hand, was a good head taller, and slender, like his mother had been. He also had her eyes, her nose, her full lips. What he didn't have was her always gentle smile. Sometimes, when Franklin smiled, it was like looking at a man who had four aces in one hand and a straight razor in the other. And you never knew which one he was going to put on the table.

At thirty-one, the kid too often looked fifty. His twin sister, much to Franklin's disgust, looked barely out of her teens.

Children, like progress, weren't always what they were cracked up to be.

Still, except for the business, they were all he had

left. God help him, he loved them both equally, and if they would only lighten up a little, lose some of the starch in their spines, they might even be friends.

He stretched and groaned with pleasure, blinking when he realized he still held the cigarette. He looked at his watch; two and a half hours. Not bad. He reached for the gold lighter on the marble-top end table.

"Father," Franklin warned.

Blaine hesitated, looked at the lighter, the telephone, and said, "The hell with it." He lit the cigarette and made a great show of inhaling, blowing a smoke ring, and grinning at the displeasure on his son's face.

"The doctor," Franklin added, too little, too late.

"The doctor," Blaine said, crossing his legs at the ankles, "doesn't want me to eat meat anymore, either. Screw him. Screw them all," He took another puff, while his left hand touched the center of his breast. "If I'm going, I'm going my way, damnit."

"Don't talk like that," Franklin snapped. "You know we don't like you talking like that."

Blaine rose and went to the curtained French doors. Outside a light fog blurred the city's lights just enough to threaten a headache if he stared at them too long. He'd go out on the balcony, but the kid would have a fit and insist he wear a coat. In the middle of October, for God's sake.

"Call downstairs," he said without turning around. "I'm hungry."

"Father, this is the Towers. We do have a kitchen, you know."

"You can cook?"

Franklin muttered something that sounded like an obscene no.

"Then call them. I want a steak and salad."

Franklin sighed loudly, deliberately; the martyr's sigh that made Blaine smile to himself. "Father, please. It's half past nine. You won't get any sleep."

I hardly sleep anyway, Blaine thought, smile gone, lifting his shoulders against an abrupt weight of melancholy.

Without a word he opened the door and stepped outside, into a curious blend of distant sound and nearby silence. Although it was warm, too warm, the humidity gave the air a touch of a chill. It almost made him shiver.

Ghost town, he thought as he looked out over the city; I'm staying in a ghost town.

The gauzy curtains on the doors softened the living-room light, made the potted shrubs along the wall seem larger and fuller than they were. He looked east, west, and smoked the cigarette to the filter before flicking it over the wall.

Franklin came out behind him.

"She loved it here," Blaine said quietly, struggling to keep a quaver from his voice. "She'll be thirty-three tomorrow, you know."

Franklin's hand rested on his shoulder; he didn't say a word.

He didn't have to.

Blaine knew what he was thinking: she's dead, Father. Thirteen years. Celeste is dead, let her go.

The lights blurred even more, and he rubbed his face hard with the heels of his hands, hoping the boy wouldn't notice that he wiped his eyes as well.

A whisper: "Father? Let's go inside."

"She hates that name. Celeste. After my mother." His hands bunched into helpless fists. "As soon as she comes home, I'm going to let her change it. I swear to God, she can call herself Spike for all I care, as long as she comes home safely."

The hand on his shoulder tightened, and tugged a little.

"Father, come on. Maybe you should rest."

He sagged and bowed his head, let his son bring him in, let him close the doors and lock them. Let him begin to turn the lamps off one by one while he stood there, a tired old man in a silly dressing gown and slippers he wouldn't throw away. Not because he was too cheap, but because his wife had given them to him on the wedding anniversary before she died, eleven years ago.

He inhaled slowly, and straightened his spine.

"Franklin," he said, "it's too damn dark in here. Turn on some lights."

"But—"

Blaine dropped into his chair and picked up the television's remote control. "The steak, Franklin, the steak. I'm not eating it in the dark."

"Father, please don't do this."

"Do what?" He aimed the remote, and the wide-screen TV snapped on. "I'm going to eat, watch a movie, and goddamnit, if Proctor doesn't answer his goddamn phone by the time I'm done, I'm going to drive over to Jersey myself and drag the son of a bitch out of bed."

The telephone rang, and no one picked it up.

*   *   *

Shake Waldman stared at the pay phone as if will alone would force the man to answer. He listened to the burring ring ten times, fifteen, before giving up. But he didn't let go of the receiver. Maybe the guy was in the shower, or watching TV, or had someone in his bed. Maybe he ought to try again, the answering machine was obviously off-line or busted.

It's only quarter to ten, try again.

Or maybe—

He closed his eyes tightly, trying to think, but the metallic clatter of the slot machines, the constant voices, the muffled music, were driving him nuts. He had to think, and he couldn't do it in here.

He wound his way quickly through the casino, keeping his gaze on the floor until he reached the relative quiet of the huge lobby. Only then did he allow himself to look back, toward the arches on the left, roped off from the main floor by red velvet. The high rollers worked those tables, when the dealers were women in black evening gowns. Tonight was the first time in years he had sat in, knowing instantly as he had before that he was in well over his head.

A couple of hands, and he was gone.

But not before he had heard the men talking.

A rolling shriek of laughter from a small group near the registration desk made him jump, and he nearly ran outside, cursing when he realized that the storm hadn't ended.

Steady rain, but small drops, with a slight wind that pushed the drops into streaks and clouds of mist that drifted over the beach, sometimes so slowly they didn't seem a part of the storm. At his back the casinos did their gaudy best to push the night away, but even without the rain they couldn't do it. The glow almost always stopped halfway across the sand.

Beyond, out of the dark, the surf rose and crested, slamming at the beach and tearing it away.

He wore a trench coat, water-stained and wrinkled, collar up, what was left of his hair covered by a duffer's cap with a beak that had long since lost its snap. The umbrella in his right hand barely kept him dry, but it allowed him to stay out in the storm without drowning on his feet.

He shifted against the railing, the cold upper bar pressing into his stomach.

He didn't know what to do.

He was pretty sure those men didn't know him. After all, he was a nobody. A gambler. Not great, but good enough not to react when he heard Proctor's name, heard the whispers and the humorless laughter. But one of them, a heavyset man in a tailored tuxedo, had watched him closely as Shake left, bidding him a sardonic good-night.

Damn, he thought; damn.

The rail quivered.

He looked sharply to his right and smiled in relief. "You want to drown, lady?"

She wore a trench coat as well, but hers fit well and reached all the way to her slender ankles. Dark leather gloves, no hat, her dark hair short and curled around her ears. One of those tiny umbrellas that were fashionable and smart and wouldn't cover a baby's shoulders.

"Taking a break, Shake, that's all." Her voice was smooth, with only a hint of the rasping that made men want to listen to her all night long. "What about you?"

He shrugged. "Downtime, that's all. Guys are talking gibberish. I think one of the damn jacks winked at me."

He couldn't see her whole profile; her collar was too high. A pale smear as they watched the Atlantic dragon try to gnaw its way to them.

"Then lay off the cards," she said simply. A hand as pale as her face touched a pocket. "Move on. Now, the dice are sexy."

He grunted a laugh. "No, Pet, *you're* sexy. The dice should be so hot. If they were, I could retire in the morning, go to Phoenix and bitch about the heat."

She nodded at the compliment, nothing more.

Lightning forked over the water, too distant to hear the split and crackle. The thunder was little more than a rumbling under the sand.

A sudden gust made him duck his head to protect his face. When he looked up again she hadn't moved, and it spooked him that he could only see one eye. It wasn't looking at him.

"Going to move on, Shake," she said at last, pulling the umbrella down, so close to her head that now there really was only just the eye. "I'm getting stale."

Maybe, he thought, I should tell her what I heard.

He passed a hand under his nose to forestall a sneeze.

"All these old folks, they're making me nervous." She laughed a little. "Sometimes they win more than me, a good sign to get out before I end up blueing my hair and trying on support hose."

Neither he nor Petra Haslic were high rollers by

any stretch of the imagination; but they weren't members of the crowds that were bused in every day either, pension checks cashed or credit cards at the ready, or that drove in for a show and a few pulls of the bandit's arm.

They were pros, without the flash and dash, the tuxes and the pearls.

A shadow world, where they earned just enough to keep a clean set of rooms and pretty good clothes and a few bucks in the bank. Not experts at anything. Jacks-of-all-trades, not really needing to be masters of anything. Enough savvy to know when a table got cold, not so much that they could walk in, sit down, walk away with thousands. Enough smarts to know when to move on, to keep the casinos from getting antsy.

Practically invisible.

Which is why, sometimes, they heard things.

"Where you headed?"

A shrug without moving. "I don't know. Dakota, maybe, or Mississippi and do the riverboat thing. I don't know."

There wasn't much else to say. He and Pet, and the others, they weren't really friends. They saw each other now and then, hung around, went to bed once in a while, sat in a bar away from the games and told stories that made them laugh or shake their heads.

He would miss her.

Lightning pointed the way to the horizon, a single bolt from sky to water.

Suddenly she touched his arm, leaned over and kissed his cheek. Whispered, "Take care, Shake, don't stay too long, you'll catch cold."

He couldn't move. He could only nod, and not look around when she walked away, the sound of her feet lost in the sound of the rain and the wind that had begun to gather to itself some strength.

He watched the waves, watched the rain, and suddenly pushed away from the railing and began to run.

He would tell her. It wouldn't do any good, but he would tell her so he wouldn't have to carry it all alone.

And if nothing happened, then nothing happened.

If he was nuts, then what the hell, he was nuts.

But he had to tell someone.

Just in case.

The telephone rang twice, then stopped.

It rang again, and someone answered by saying, "It's late."

"I know," said Falcon, "and I am sorry, really. We left the phone machine off, and I was concerned, that's all. I apologize for the intrusion."

"Thanks, Doc. I appreciate it."

"Well. All right then. One thing though—was it bad?"

"Yes," said Ethan Proctor, "it was bad."

And he hung up.

FIVE

The October mist on the Hudson didn't last very long. But while it did, nothing moved.

Anywhere.

No cars on the street, no planes in the air, and if there were boats down there, they were hidden. Across the river, apartment towers were dark, their western faces still in shadow.

It happened every morning; and every morning, for that one brief moment, Proctor always wondered where everyone had gone.

He sat on the deck, feet propped against the railing, sunglasses in place against the climbing sun, and held a mug of hot chocolate close to his chest. The edge of the cliff was only fifteen feet away, masked by low yew and hemlock deliberately maintained to spread and thicken to hide the rocks, but not the water.

A scrabbling beneath him brought a smile.

The deck was only a foot above the ground, just high enough for the neighborhood squirrels to use the gap beneath as a racecourse, and a way to escape whatever marauders were still around.

"Quiet down," he scolded mildly. "This is a Zen moment here."

The scrabbling didn't stop.

He inhaled deeply, smelling evergreen and damp grass; he sipped, and tasted, as usual, too much cocoa; he yawned so hard he nearly choked. The smile again. A half smile. Few had ever seen both sides of his mouth pull back at the same time.

With a low grunt he leaned forward and set the mug on the top rail and stretched with hands clasped over his head, content at the pull of the muscles, the faint pop of his left shoulder. When he reached the point of pain, he lowered his arms until they dangled at his sides, and the blood tingled into his fingertips as he flexed them.

He supposed, since it was now well past nine, that it was about time to get to work; he supposed, since he was the boss, he could get to work anytime he wanted to.

Not that there was all that much to do.

He had already read Taz's report and decided this one was for the police. Lozario would be in no mood for anything else. Other than that, all the others' active cases were within a day or two of closing.

Most of Black Oak's investigations dealt with what Doc liked to call involuntary depletion of financial resources due to unexpected outlets of opportunity. Scams, Proctor called them bluntly; they didn't deserve something that sounded at the same time so bland and so grand. Nothing more than scams. Initiated by people who believed they had found a way to beat a company's system, either by stealing money or parts or ideas or a business's future plans.

A much smaller percentage of his work dealt with

scams of other sorts—from fortune-tellers and for-
tune hunters.

The last involved finding people. Runaways, lost
parents, lost children, lost childhood, lost memories.

In all cases, it was not automatic that the police,
or the appropriate state or federal authorities, were
contacted. It depended on those involved. There was,
in his mind, a vast difference between greed of all
kinds, and desperations in the same number. Sometimes restitution was all that was required; sometimes not even that.

And sometimes Proctor wanted to shoot the son of
a bitch and save everyone the trouble.

Whatever the disposition, no matter what the others said, it always came down to his call.

He grabbed the mug and drank, winced at the
lukewarm liquid, and finished it quickly before set-
ting the mug on the deck beside his chair.

The squirrels were gone; the mist long gone. An
airliner coasted under the sun toward LaGuardia. A
sight-seeing boat chugged upriver toward West
Point.

The living room's screen door opened, and Lana
said, "You do know, of course, that the phones and
fax are out again."

The advantage of having a dense screen of mature
blue spruce around the property was that neighbors
and passersby rarely had more than a glimpse of the
elongated ranch house that lay behind it; the disad-
vantage, as Lana had pointed out to him on innumer-
able occasions, was his refusal to evict any critters
that decided to make the trees their home. Including

one family of blond-tailed squirrels which, once or twice a year, actively resented the telephone lines that poked through the branches.

Proctor didn't move beyond a gesture that was a cross between *no, I didn't know* and *you know what to do.*

She muttered, "Impossible," and went back inside; not, however, without slamming the screen door a little to let him know how she felt. This was not part of her job description. His house, his phone lines, his damn squirrels. Not hers.

He grinned as the scrabbling started again beneath the deck.

"Tomahawk's out, boys," he said. "Stay out of sight."

"And quit talking to them," she yelled.

This time he laughed. But silently. Lana Kelaleha was not a woman to tempt too far. One of his greatest fears was that she would find someplace else to work; replacing her, he suspected, would be impossible. She was both investigator and de facto office manager. Her expertise lay in computers; while he knew how to work them, she knew the magic.

A few minutes later she dumped a pile of envelopes on the table. "Mail call."

"Phones?"

"On their way."

She turned to go.

"Sit a while."

"I'm busy, Proctor. It's Thursday, remember? RJ isn't coming in until noon, but I want to start catching up on the reports."

"Humor me."

She hesitated, and it took a second for him to realize why: the deck ran from the living room's north wall thirty feet down the back of the house. The only other chair was outside a sliding glass door that led into his bedroom.

It was as if a solid oak door were on the outside as well.

With a nod he told her it was all right, but she almost ran anyway, as if there be dragons down there.

Proctor's territory.

Proctor's dragons.

He had stopped being concerned about the reaction a long time ago.

A small concession: he turned his chair around so they would face the window, not the sun. The sky was just hazed enough so there was no glare.

They spent the rest of the time until noon doing what he hated most—the minutiae of Black Oak. Billings, signing checks and depositions, and answering, into a tape recorder for RJ to transcribe later, letters of thanks or regret, from those the company served. By the time RJ arrived, take-out Chinese in hand, breathless and giggling over something her boyfriend had said, he was ready for lunch. And the next phase.

After eating, he and Lana took turns opening the mail. Requests for services, requests for information, pleas for assistance. There were also transcribed messages taken from the phone machine, as well as the tapes themselves.

As usual, RJ sat cross-legged on the deck, keeping her comments to herself, although he could tell by the tilt of her head what she thought of some of what she heard.

When they were done, she left for her office. Not a word. Not a single word. RitaJane always made sure the others knew that she knew her place.

"So?" Lana stared at the pile on the table. "What do you think?"

"I think she'll be married by the end of the year, or he's going to dump her and we'll have to get someone else because her funk will make her useless."

"Besides that."

He closed his eyes, and slumped until he could rest his head on the chair's back. His feet braced against the window's narrow outer ledge, knees bent, hands resting on his thighs.

"Offhand? I don't see anything very promising there. It's the same old stuff."

"Oh, Lord," she said to the air. "He's bored."

"But it's true."

He had done work for companies as large as General Motors and as small as a corner grocery; the scams didn't change, only the size of the victims. Not, he reminded himself before she did, that their post office box was exactly overflowing with potential customers these days.

She would also remind him that the "same old stuff" is what paid the bills. And her salary.

Not to mention the fact that even the "same old stuff" was getting a little scarce these days. The steadily increasing availability of security systems and gadgets, once relegated to spy movies and TV, had taken some of the mystique from Black Oak, and others like it. Why hire a spy when you can do the spying yourself? For less money.

He tilted his head to look at her.

She looked back and scowled. "What?"

"Nothing. Just looking."

"Well, knock it off."

He shrugged and looked away, back at the window, at the reflections he saw there.

Lana—a short, just shy of pudgy, woman made oddly attractive as a result of a burly Mexican father and slender Polynesian mother, who had met while the former had been on shore leave in Hawaii. It was an exotic combination, and a powerful one when her targets refused to understand that behind those square bangs and short black hair was someone who would just as easily gut them as flirt with them.

He had a feeling that twenty years from now, when she was in her mid-sixties, the only difference would be that she'd be crankier than ever.

And himself . . . he frowned.

All he could see was the sandy hair that once in a while sprouted a bizarre streak of dark brown or vivid auburn off one temple or the other, depending on how much time he had spent in the sun. Longer than an insurance salesman's, shorter than those still stuck in their youth, with an unruly arc that dipped down over his forehead, and a part that was never in the same place twice.

He couldn't see his face.

"Proctor, are you all right?"

He sat up and leaned forward, squinting.

He couldn't see his face.

"Proctor?"

The pane was too far for him to reach with a finger, but he tried anyway, failed, and slumped back.

She touched his shoulder.

"A ghost," he said lightly, pointing to the window. "I'm a ghost."

"Oh. Okay. So . . . Casper or Captain Kidd?"

"Ah. Friendly, or a murderous pirate. Hell of a choice."

He supposed she would choose the pirate.

He leaned forward again, and this time saw the dark eyebrows and deep-set eyes floating in the glass. Below them should have been an ordinary, lightly tanned face whose once-severe angles had softened over the years, even though he was only a decade younger than she.

It wasn't there.

This, he thought, is too damn weird, and he scraped his chair around until he faced the river.

Sunglasses back in place; legs crossed, right ankle resting on left knee.

"The others," he said quietly, a little hoarsely, and held out his hand.

One by one she handed over the letters, without comment.

They were forwarded by contacts, most of whom he had never met in person but had, in one capacity or another, worked with at one time or another.

The answers, if there were any, would be fed back through those same contacts.

Unless he decided to act on his own.

A haunting in Indiana, a spate of nightlights over Oregon, a werewolf in Baton Rouge, a zombie in Des

Moines, a saucer crash in Iowa, crop circles every-
where, and a woman who wanted her daughter back
from Mars so she could graduate from college.

"Where the hell is Delany?" he said, dropping each
letter unanswered onto the table.

"Tomorrow night, maybe Saturday morning," she
reminded him.

"That long?" He groaned. "Whose bright idea was
it to give him three weeks anyway?"

"You were the one who said he was working himself to death."

"He's the same age as Doc."

"Doc takes care of himself. Delany," she said, cocking a plucked eyebrow at him, "lives on junk food
and sugar."

"Every civilization has its ambrosia. Who's to say
that a rich chocolate shake, a real hamburger, and
fries that aren't soggy isn't ours?"

"I do."

"Ah. Well, there you go, then." He turned his
head. "How did Taz do with the picture?"

He didn't move when the shadow of the house
began to slide across the deck. There would be a chill
soon, and he welcomed it, hoping it would prod his
mind out of the funk it had been in since the night
before.

Just like almost every Wednesday night, and almost every Thursday.

A glance at the now-empty table, still seeing the
letters Lana had taken with her—her turn to word
the regrets. Sometimes he envied those people, the

haunted and the abducted and the terrified by monsters. It was perverse, and he understood that. But at least, in the moment of their terror or their longing, they believed.

They believed in something so strongly, however fleetingly, that their lives would never be the same for it.

His own reputation, quiet but pervasive, was that of an open-minded skeptic. A debunker who scrupulously avoided publicity. A relentless, sometimes ruthless, exposer of charlatans and jackals who preyed on the helpless and hapless. The one who explained that even those who seemed to actually believe in the cards they read or the spirits they spoke to were only victims themselves, not genuine recipients of the truth.

He didn't take many of those cases, and he rarely accepted money when he did. They were too often too easy; even the difficult ones were ultimately disappointing in the simplicity of their designs.

But once in a while he failed.

That wasn't surprising; he knew that sometimes he thought himself more clever than he really was, which inevitably led to a falling on his face after tripping over his own ego.

That didn't mean the case in question was the real thing.

Except . . .

. . . *a cold night in December, and just enough snow to cover the grass.*

A full moon.

A strong wind.
And a man standing on the lawn . . .

Proctor closed his eyes tightly and held his breath.
The shade hadn't reached him, but he felt the chill
just the same.

SIX

All he knew was that he was on a narrow bed, a thin short quilt drawn midway up his chest, exposing his feet. His shoes were off, but not the rest of his clothes. His arms and legs were strapped down, but not so tightly that he couldn't move them a little to keep the circulation going.

All he knew was that the sun was up, the blurred glare of it outlining drapes pulled over the single window on the wall to his left. Thursday, he reckoned, but no telling how early or late.

Between his stocking feet he could make out the dim form of a low, unremarkable dresser against the opposite wall, a simple mirror hanging over it that reflected the blank wall above his head. The wall on his right was white-pine-paneled from floor to ceiling; he wasn't sure but he thought he could make out a doorknob—closet or exit he didn't know.

All he knew was that the figure at the end of the long table had moved impossibly swiftly when he tried to kick the chair back and stand.

don't kill him

Hands had grabbed his arms and pinned them to his sides; hands had lifted him off his feet without effort; the body had twisted around and the hands had slammed him onto the table.

He hit his head, and the light had turned black.

He didn't remember being carried, nor being strapped down. By the feel of it, he didn't think he'd been drugged; his skull just felt as if it had been introduced to a baseball bat. He supposed, then, that the daze he had been in had soon carried over into sleep. An escape.

He just wished he had been able to see the face of the man who had manhandled him so easily. But he had only seen Maggie's face, briefly, just a glimpse of a rueful, apologetic smile as she'd stepped out of the way.

Son of a bitch, he thought angrily; son of a goddamn bitch.

A man of his age, his experience, caught in one of the oldest tricks in the book. What the hell had he been thinking of, anyway, flirting with her like that, knowing damn well she was feeding him nonsense.

The guy was probably her husband.

Damn, but he felt stupid. Proctor was going to skin him alive when he found out.

don't kill him

He listened for a while, but couldn't hear anything but his own breathing until, some minutes later, the growl of a small truck grew and faded. Which didn't tell him much, not even where he was. He could be in one of the cabins, or a room in the main building.

Not that it mattered.

He was caught well and good and still feeling like a fool.

"So now what?" he asked the ceiling.

If they hadn't done so already, Maggie and her partner, whoever the hell he was, would go through his things, get mad because they wouldn't find a whole hell of a lot of money, and eventually get around to trying to find out if he was worth money to someone else.

If they were dumb, they'd use the ATM card or his credit card, getting what cash they could and leaving a way to trace him; if they were smart, they'd just kill him, no matter what Maggie said.

His stomach burbled, and he wanted something to drink.

He tried to sit up, but his arms were spread too wide. The best he could do was lift his shoulders off the mattress a couple of inches. So much, he thought sourly, for jumping whoever came through the door first.

What an idiot.

What, as Bugs would say, a maroon.

So much for your scintillating Irish charm, Delany.

He groaned his disgust and flexed his knees to see if he could pull his feet through the straps' loops.

When the left one almost made it, he had to bite down on his lower lip to keep from shouting. A smug grin, a deep breath, and a reminder that freeing a foot wasn't going to do him much good. What he needed was a hand, and unless he had lost it entirely, the right one just might make it.

All he needed was a little time, and a lot of luck.

Lana and RJ were gone, and he was alone.

Hands in pockets, he wandered down the hall, peering into Rita's office on the left, into Lana's on the right with her computers mute and blind, the printer silent, the bookshelves neat, each section labeled underneath. The other two rooms were a full bathroom, and a storage room whose arrangement only the two women understood.

But they weren't here to explain. Doc was in the city still at work on a case, and Taz wasn't due in again until Monday.

He scratched the back of his head; he rubbed his left shoulder with his right hand; he returned to the living room and wondered if he could kill time putting something in the microwave and eat while he watched something on TV.

Kill time.

Lana was right—he was bored.

Even as he sat on the sofa and picked up the remote, he knew what would happen: he would start at the first channel and cycle his way through everything the rooftop satellite dish had to offer. Pausing here and there. Watching nothing to its conclusion. Always coming in on the last second of a news story he might have found interesting if he'd only found it sooner.

He didn't bother to turn the set on; he didn't bother to go into the kitchen.

He looked down the hall into the place that was his home.

Nothing tempted him there, either.

He sat back and watched the window sprout droplets that shimmied their way down the pane to the sill.

He could always close the drapes, but that would make the room too dark; he could get off his duff, get in the car, and go for a drive, but that would require conscious thought and effort; he could even give Taz a call, congratulate him on a job well-done, and see if the kid had any plans for the day off Proctor had given him.

He grunted.

Sure. A good-looking guy like that? If Taz didn't have a hundred women just waiting for him to show up, he'd quit the business and grow tomatoes for a living.

When the telephone rang, he almost lunged toward it.

"Mr. Proctor? Ethan Proctor?"

He didn't recognize the voice; a man, nothing more.

"Speaking."

"Mr. Proctor. I apologize for bothering you, but I represent Mr. Taylor Blaine."

Proctor shrugged, and waited.

The man cleared his throat. "We—that is, my father and I, I am Franklin Blaine . . . we wish to consult with you on a matter of some importance to my father."

Proctor stared blindly at the window as the man went on, saying the same thing in several different ways. It didn't make any difference. He heard reluctance there, and a clear indication that this man was making the call against his better judgment.

Proctor finally interrupted him with, "About what, Mr. Blaine?"

"My sister."

"What about her?"

"She's missing, Mr. Proctor, and my father wants you to find her."

Proctor shifted uneasily. *My father wants you.* Not *we want you.* Not a good sign. And he wasn't so desperate that he needed to get involved in a family's civil war.

Still: "I assume you've already alerted the police, Mr. Blaine?"

"The police, sir, gave up a long time ago."

Proctor frowned. "Why is that?"

"She's been gone for thirteen years, Mr. Proctor."

All the warning signals went up at once, especially the one that shrilled obsession.

This was definitely out of the question.

"I'm sorry, Mr. Blaine," he said regretfully, "but I'm a little too busy these days to take on a new case. Especially, if you don't mind me saying so, one as old as this."

"I don't mind at all, Mr. Proctor, and I thank you for your time."

The phone went dead.

Proctor held the receiver a moment longer, then replaced it as he mimed wiping sweat from his brow. Obsession and family warfare, and the clear relief he had heard in the man's voice at the refusal.

Definitely something he did not need.

Which left him now with the same problem as before: what to do with the rest of his day.

It wasn't so much that he hadn't the imagination to think of something as it was the fact that he wasn't used to so much inactivity for so long a time.

A glance down the office hallway made him feel slightly guilty. Maybe he shouldn't have turned

Blaine down so quickly, or at least not without consulting the others. There had been the sound of privilege in the man's voice, and that usually meant money. If the father was still looking for a daughter lost that long, the fee would be—

"Screw it."

The house was getting to him; it was time to see what the outside world had to offer.

He'd think about Blaine later. If he thought about him at all.

Shake huddled in a phone booth, his heel pressed against the door so it wouldn't open. Although he was pretty sure he hadn't been followed, he couldn't resist glancing over his shoulder every few seconds, watching the corner store's entrance, holding his breath every time someone came in.

He had been this way all day.

It was driving him nuts.

No one knew him. Certainly not those high rollers he had overheard. He was a nobody. A nothing. A ghost, for God's sake.

Yet he hadn't been able to shake the feeling that someone was watching. Just out of sight. Just around the corner.

All day.

All damn day.

He had slept with his clothes on, a chair and the chest of drawers shoved against the door, the umbrella in his right hand to use as a weapon. Useless, of course; totally useless, but it was all he had.

From dawn until now he had walked, avoiding the casinos, keeping to the side streets, trying to figure out what he should do next. What he had heard he'd scribbled on a piece of paper and given to Pet. She hadn't said anything, only put it in her purse and walked away. No kiss this time. She just walked away.

"Come on," he whispered to the phone. "Come on, man, come on, I ain't got all day."

What he would do was, he would get the first bus out, head south, maybe to Atlanta or Birmingham. Then go as far west as he could before the ocean stopped him. After that he would find a new line of work, become a different kind of ghost and disappear for good.

They didn't know who he was, but he couldn't help the feeling.

Someone was out there.

They knew exactly where he was.

The ringing stopped, he stiffened, and mouthed a vicious curse when he heard the answering machine run its spiel.

Shit, shit, what do I—

"Hey, Mr. Proctor? Shake Waldman, down in Atlantic City? Ain't seen you in a couple of years, but we been talking, right? I, uh, damn I hate these things . . . I, uh, I got some news I think you ought to know. You can't call me, I'm on the move, I'll have to call you back."

He closed his eyes, took a breath.

"Don't go anywhere, Mr. Proctor. Please. Please stick around. I need to talk to you, man. I need to talk bad."

He hung up, and rested his forehead against the dial, feeling he was either going to throw up or faint.

When it passed, he automatically fingered the change slot, just in case, and left. He averted his face so the clerk wouldn't see him; he swung immediately to the right so the clerk wouldn't see him through the window; he walked away from the boardwalk, grateful there was still a mist in the air, allowing him to use the umbrella without suspicion.

But he checked every car that passed him.

He watched the feet of every pedestrian who walked by, so he would recognize the shoes again.

He kept his right hand in his trench-coat pocket, squeezing the roll of money he had taken from his room. Nothing else. No clothes, no books, no toiletries, no nothing. Just the cash.

He wandered until his legs began to tremble, and he began to mutter to them, begging them to hang on until he reached the bus station. He'd call Proctor from there, and if the guy still didn't answer, then the hell with him, he was gone.

His legs didn't listen.

He was on Atlantic, a wide boulevard of an avenue that ran parallel to the beach through the center of town. The old-timers, they told him it used to be a great place, with really nice stores and friendly shops and lots of people. That must have been a hundred years ago, because it looked like hell now, and most of the people he saw were hookers who looked just as bad.

A cramp seized his right calf, and he moaned and went down on one knee, the umbrella wobbling as he tried to use the same hand to brace himself against a city trash receptacle. Tears blinded him for a mo-

ment, and he could feel the cold damp concrete
under his knee.

"Trouble, fella?"

He blinked the tears away and looked up.

A guy in a nice coat, collar up, hair slick with mist.

"Cramp," he said.

The man reached down and took his elbow. "Here,
come on."

Shake felt the grip and rose slowly, nearly losing
his balance, and nearly poking the guy's eye out with
the umbrella. "Sorry."

"No problem. You going to be okay?"

Shake tested the leg and nodded. "Yeah. Think
so. Thanks."

A car pulled up to the curb. The back door opened.

"You need a lift?"

"Nope. Thanks, though."

He frowned, then. The man was different somehow, and it took a second before Shake realized
why—the man's left eye was false. It didn't follow
the other's tracking, and it looked . . . he almost
giggled . . . it looked like a marble. A green-and-
white tiger's-eye marble.

"Thanks," he said again. "I'll be okay."

"Like I said, no problem." The man still had his
elbow. "The thing is, though, Mr. Waldman, is that
you really shouldn't play for high stakes when you
can't afford to lose, you know?" He smiled, briefly.
"Gamble with your head, not over it. You know what
I mean?"

Shake saw the hand fall away.

He saw the man get into the car.

He saw the dead eye, staring.

He saw the gun as the door closed.

Broad daylight, he thought; for God's sake, it's broad daylight.

One step back was all he was given.

The next thing he knew, he was staring at the clouds and feeling the mist on his face as the sun set too early.

Someone began to cry.

He hoped it wasn't him.

SEVEN

"Honey, I'm home!" Proctor called as he stepped into the kitchen, locking the screen and inner doors behind him. He knew that an answer would turn his hair instantly from sandy to snowy, assuming he survived the heart attack that came first; but there were nights, like tonight, when he really got tired of listening to his own voice.

A sandwich, a long drive, and a couple of drinks, wandering home after midnight . . . that did it to him every time.

He ought to know better, but he never learned.

"Last chance," he called. And rolled his eyes.

A small bulb burned under the stove's hood, just bright enough to let him get to the living room without cracking a shin. Once there he settled for switching on one end-table lamp as he shrugged off his coat and tossed it over the back of an armchair.

The red light on the answering machine winked three times. He sat heavily on the couch and stared at it for a few seconds. It was late, almost midnight, and he wasn't sure he was awake enough to pay proper attention. Besides, it couldn't be anything that wouldn't wait until morning.

He sighed loudly.

Of course it could.

One of the nursing-home doctors, one of the nurses.

It never had been before. But it could be now.

Mom, he thought; Mom.

It could also be Delany, home a day early and ready to show off the junk he had gathered.

"Yeah," he muttered. "Right."

He pressed the "play" button, grabbed a pad and pen from the coffee table, and sat back.

A strong voice, lightly rough:

"Mr. Proctor, this is Taylor Blaine. You spoke to my son earlier, I believe, and I'm told you have rejected our offer. I would prefer to speak to you personally about this matter, as soon as you have appropriate free time. This is not a frivolous request, Mr. Proctor. And I am not . . . what's the phrase? Tilting at windmills? I want my daughter back. I will, one way or another, do anything to see that it happens. I will be at the Waldorf Towers all weekend. At least give me the courtesy of a return call."

Proctor hit the "pause" button and shook his head. He felt for the man. He had his own loss to shoulder, had felt it every day of his life for the past five years, and he believed he understood Blaine's reaction to the refusal.

He also knew that empathy wasn't always a wise basis upon which to accept a case.

He hit the button for the next message.

*   *   *

"Blaine, again, Mr. Proctor. I forget to mention that I am well aware of your enviable reputation, and I am equally aware of your current business situation. Work with me on this, Mr. Proctor, and it will be a long time before you have to worry about bills again."

Again Proctor hit the "pause" button. He leaned back and stared at the night black window, a hand cupped around his chin.

There had been no arrogance in the man's voice, and no command for an appearance. He wasn't at all sure he appreciated the fact that Blaine had investigated him, although it was a point in the man's favor—that Black Oak hadn't been simply picked out of the yellow pages.

Blaine had been matter-of-fact. Not even the "enviable reputation" had been flattery. Proctor suspected the guy had never sucked up to anyone in his life.

Neither did he think the offer had been a boast.

Not worry about bills for a long time.

Nice. It would be nice.

As much for the others as for himself.

He tapped the pen thoughtfully against the pad and let the tape run to the last message.

"Hey, Mr. Proctor? Shake Waldman, down in Atlantic City? Ain't seen you in a couple of years, but we been talking, right? I, uh, damn I hate these things . . ."

Proctor smiled as he listened. A blast from the past; just what he needed.

Then:

"Don't go anywhere, Mr. Proctor. Please. Please stick around. I need to talk to you, man. I need to talk bad."

"Ah, Shake," he said as he removed the tape from the machine. "What have you gotten yourself into now?"

Although Waldman was a low-level professional gambler, Proctor knew the man skated a little too close to the edge sometimes. This sounded an awful lot like a preliminary hit for a loan to rebuild his stake. He had probably lost a bundle and the sharks were circling.

Miss America or not, Atlantic City was no place to get in over your head with the boys who really mattered.

And the boys were people he definitely had no interest in getting to know. He had gotten a lot of people mad at him in his time, and he didn't need to get that bunch ticked at him too.

For one thing, Doc would strangle him, if Lana didn't get to him first.

He shook his head and brought the tape into RJ's office for safekeeping, replaced it with a new one and watched CNN for half an hour. Same old news, same old sports.

When Shake didn't call again, he went to bed, thinking he should probably talk to Lana about Blaine in the morning. Unless Delany came home first, in which case all bets for the time being were off.

* * *

. . . a cold night in December, and just enough snow to cover the grass.

A full moon.

A strong wind.

And a man standing on the lawn, just at the edge of the kitchen-window light.

The rest of the house is dark.

Proctor stands at the dining-room window. Staring. Not believing.

The man wears a camel's hair topcoat, unbuttoned, collar up, his hands in the pockets. His sparse white hair rises and twists, and falls with the wind. His cheeks are full, the cold giving them color. Stray snowflakes dance around him, but not one of them lands.

Proctor rubs his face hard, rubs his eyes until they hurt, leans as close to the pane as he can get.

Then the man on the lawn looks up . . .

And Proctor sat up abruptly, swallowing hard, shivering as the sweat that covered his face and torso met the bedroom air.

"Damn," he whispered. "Damn."

It was the first time in a long time that the dream had come to him while he slept. Usually he could just close his eyes and see it all, and feel the cold both in the house and out.

Because it wasn't, in the end, any dream at all.

"Brother."

Slowly he swung his legs over the edge of the mattress and sat for a while, waiting until he was sure the dream was gone. A yawn overtook him, halfhearted at best, and a glance at the clock radio on the nightstand made him wince. He trudged over to the sliding glass door and yanked open the heavy drapes.

The horizon was light, bleaching night from the sky.

He sighed, yawned again, and stared longingly at the bed. But there was no sense now trying to get more sleep. All he would do is lie there, staring at the ceiling . . . and thinking too damn much.

He wondered then what had awakened him. Every other time, he had ridden the dream-memory to its inevitable conclusion. Which wasn't all that frightening.

His smile was crooked.

Except, he reminded himself, for that first time.

On that cold night in December.

He grabbed a bathrobe and slipped it on, scratching his hair and chest sleepily as he wandered out of the room and up the hall. Something had interrupted him, but he couldn't figure out what. No water dripped in the bathroom, he had no pets and it was almost but not quite time for the squirrels and birds, and no one had stayed over.

He yawned, rubbed his eyes again, and opened the heavy oak door.

The red light winked on the answering machine.

He couldn't move, and he didn't want to breathe.

No call this late, this early, could possibly be good news.

And the first thing he thought was: *Mom has died.*

He couldn't move.

He didn't want to move.

He had seen her only two nights ago, and she had been fine. All things considered, she had been okay. Physically, that is. Even the doctors were pleased with her, and the nurses had no complaints because she never caused them any trouble.

How could she die? Just the other night, for God's sake; it was just the other night.

He shuffled over to the couch and sat, hands between his legs.

The light winked.

He stared at it, afraid of it, aware of something deeply cold and heavy expanding in his stomach.

"Press the damn button," he whispered to his hands.

He couldn't.

He just couldn't.

If she was dead, he would never know what had happened to make her the way she was. If she was dead, he would never learn the reason why she had—

"Damnit, press the button!"

He watched his hand reach out, watched the finger press the button, and held his breath while the tape whirred to the beginning.

Please, he thought; please.

"Proctor—"

"Goddamnit!" he yelled and jumped to his feet. "Damn you, Delany, what the hell are you doing, scaring the shit out of me like that? Are you out of your goddamn mind, you—"

He stopped.

He swallowed, and passed a trembling hand through his hair as he stared stupidly at the telephone. Frowning. Cocking his head as if he'd be able to catch Delany's words still floating around the room.

When his breathing returned to normal, when his hands stopped shaking, he sat and pressed play.

And Delany said, "Proctor, Jesus, Proctor, Crockston, it's Crockston for the love of God don't let them *Jesus!*"

A static-filled noise overwhelmed the rest—the roar of a large engine, the roar of an animal.

And something else, all too clearly:

Delany screaming.

EIGHT

Proctor couldn't move.

He stared blindly across the room at the window slowly filling with light. A stray thought: he had forgotten to draw the drapes last night.

His left heel began to bounce on the carpet, and it took a deliberate effort to stop it.

Another: it was a joke, Delany announcing he was on his way home.

Except Delany never joked like that. He told jokes, he explained jokes, but he never played practical jokes because he could never keep quiet about them, couldn't stop giggling before they played out.

Proctor gripped the lapels of his robe in one hand to protect his chest against the chill that had seeped into the room. Even the sunrise looked cold.

Another: Delany was dead.

His hands gripped his knees to stop them from trembling, to keep his heel from starting again.

Delany was dead.

He remembered to breathe.

He reached out to play the message again, and drew his hand back.

No; maybe not dead.

Delany had screamed.

Maybe not.

He inhaled again, flexing his fingers in and out of fists, ignoring the frost that had risen into his lungs. Sitting here wasn't going to solve anything, he knew it, yet calm remained just out of reach, and frustration at his sudden inability to do something, anything, made him moan aloud.

Think, he ordered; for God's sake, think.

for the love of God don't let—

He felt just like the man in the old definition of confusion, the one who jumped on his horse and rode off in all directions.

That's what he needed: one direction at a time. Scattering himself wasn't going to do Sloan any good. His eyes closed briefly, but he didn't like the dark he found back there; his hands calmed their trembling, but they didn't know what to do; his legs wanted him to stand and get moving, but they didn't know where to go.

One direction at a time.

He blew out hard, rapidly, until his lungs emptied. Then he breathed again, one long and slow inhalation, one long and slow exhalation.

The first thing he had to do was get help, get things in order. Even the cavalry had to saddle their horses.

He reached for the receiver, recoiled, then snatched it up and dialed Lana's number. After several interminable rings, a male voice answered, smothered in sleep.

"Chico, it's Proctor. Is Lana there?"

Chico Kelaleha had a first name his wife had long

ago shortened because, she claimed, it took her all day to pronounce it, and gringos never could. "Shower," he mumbled grumpily. "What the hell you calling so early for?"

"Trouble," was all Proctor said. "Have her call me back right away."

Now Chico was awake. "You need me?"

"To hold the fort, that's all."

"Wait. I'll get her."

Proctor started to protest, heard the other receiver clunk onto a table, and waited impatiently. Counting seconds. Too many seconds. Watching the light strengthen in the window. Listening to the squirrels thud across the porch, to the birds chirping too damn cheerful. Listening to Chico's deep voice whispering, listening to Lana's grow louder.

"What?" she said.

"Delany's in trouble," Proctor answered, and ignored her sharp gasp. "I don't know what, that's all I know, don't ask. He's in trouble, and I have to leave. Get here as soon as you can. I may be gone. If I am, I'll call you when I can."

"Fine," she said, and hung up.

A finger tapped on the coffee table. He wanted to get Doc to go with him wherever it was he had to go, but that would mean abandoning an important case in the city. According to the last report, Falcon was on the cusp, and pulling out now would be a disaster. He couldn't afford that; without it, paychecks would be hard to come by.

Immediately he had the thought, he winced in disgust: Delany was in obviously serious trouble, and he was worried about cash flow.

But word would get around if Doc pulled out now: reliability was everything, and Black Oak's reputation depended on it to survive.

A curse, sharp and strong, but he had no other choice. Lana was needed here, Doc in New York. He called Taz. A woman answered, and he grinned and identified himself.

"Boss," Taz said breathlessly a moment later, trying to sound professional against a background of muffled giggling. "What's up?"

"You free for the weekend?"

"I guess."

"Delany's in trouble. We have to leave town. Get here an hour ago. Packed. Light."

"But what about Lozario? The job?"

"Doc'll take care of it. Move it, Taz, I need you."

One direction at a time.

He stood, shook himself, and started for his bedroom.

A single step, before the doorbell rang.

Reaction was automatic: he tightened the robe's belt and swore his way into the kitchen. At this hour no one, not even salesmen or proselytizers, should be at his door. Which meant it had to be either so uncommonly trivial that he would lose what little grip of his temper he had left, or it would be important, although how, he couldn't possibly imagine.

He yanked open the door, scowling, and snapped, "What?"

Then he saw the long limousine in the driveway, a pastel shade of an autumn sky. Darkly tinted windows. A faint shimmer to suggest the motor was on idle.

"Mr. Proctor?"

The old man on the porch was an inch shorter than he, in a dark cashmere topcoat belted loosely at the waist.

"Mr. Proctor, I am Taylor Blaine."

Proctor shook his head in disgust. "Look, Mr. Blaine, I haven't got time for . . ." He began to shiver, and realized how he was dressed. "Oh, hell, come in, but I'm in a hurry and I don't have time for you."

He strode back into the living room, suggested the man take a seat, and hurried down the hall, making sure he closed the oak door solidly, loudly.

It doesn't rain, it doesn't pour, it goddamn floods, he thought angrily as he ducked into his bedroom and dressed—slacks and dark sports jacket, no need for a tie. No time to figure out what he needed, what he might need—in one of the two closets was a small cloth bag perpetually packed with jeans and shirts, toiletries, and a handful of other things he always took with him. Necessities; nothing more.

"A quick trip to the bathroom, a brush for his hair, and he opened the door again, startled when he found Blaine waiting on the other side.

"You wouldn't come to me, so I came to you," Blaine said amiably.

Proctor eased the man back without actually touching him and closed the door, testing to make sure it had locked itself. Then he dropped his bag on the couch, and said, "Mr. Blaine, I'm sorry, really sorry, but there's something I have to take care of, and it can't wait."

"A minute," Blaine said. "All I ask is one minute."

"If I had a minute, I'd be out of here already. Sorry."

"Trouble?"

"You could say that."

The kitchen door opened and Taz yelled, "Hey, boss, there's a humongous limo in the drive, you know that? I knocked on the window but the guy in back wouldn't—" He stopped when he saw Blaine by the stereo wall. "Oh."

Proctor gestured vaguely, almost rudely. "Taz, this is Taylor Blaine. Mr. Blaine, this is my associate, Paul Tazaretti." He pointed at the telephone. "Taz, press the button and listen. Mr. Blaine, I would appreciate it if you left now."

Blaine didn't move.

Taz sat in front of the phone and pressed the button.

Delany's voice.

Delany's screams.

Taz swallowed and looked up, pale and confused. "I—"

"Where was he?" Proctor demanded harshly. "Where the hell was he?"

Taz shook his head hopelessly. "I don't . . ." He snapped his fingers. "Wait a minute, wait a minute . . . Kentucky, I think. That picture was from Kentucky, right? Yeah. Maybe he's still there."

Proctor turned his back to the room and opened one of the bookcase doors. "Crockston . . . Crockettstown . . . Davy Crockett, probably." He nodded as he hauled out a large atlas. "Yeah. Yeah, Kentucky." He flipped the pages hard, tearing one, turned around and said, "Right. Kentucky . . . here. Near the Virginia border. The Cumberland Mountains." He closed the book and slammed it back into its place. "Let's go, Taz."

"Mr. Proctor."

It was Blaine.

Proctor grabbed Taz's shoulder and urged him to his feet, grabbed his bag and pushed him toward the kitchen. "No time, Mr. Blaine, like I told you. Like you heard. Taz, we'll take your heap, if you don't mind."

"Mr. Proctor, how do you propose to get there?"

Proctor stopped in the dining room. Blaine hadn't moved except to unbelt his coat.

"I'm sure not going to walk," Proctor said sarcastically. "Now if you don't—"

"Commercial airlines are a funny lot," Blaine said, studying the carpet at his feet. "You'll have to make at least one connection, maybe two, to get into Lexington or Frankfort. There are no nonstop flights, I guarantee it. Then you'll have to rent a car and drive the rest of the way. Or you can dance the same dance into Roanoke, or someplace else in Virginia or Tennessee. Either way, Mr. Proctor, it's going to take more time than you want." A glance at the phone. "More time than you apparently have."

Proctor knew he was right, and knew all too well what was coming.

"I can help," Blaine offered.

"Private jet?"

Blaine shrugged without modesty.

"Where?"

This time Blaine smiled. "You name it, Mr. Proctor, you name it."

He wasn't boasting.

"And the price?" Proctor said, making sure the man knew he wasn't pleased with the position he'd been put in.

Blaine stopped smiling. "I have my charities, Mr. Proctor. My children don't like it, but I have my charities." He glanced around the room and headed for the back door. "No offense, young man, but you are not one of them."

After a look to Taz, who shrugged a *why not?*, Proctor set his bag on the dining-room table and hurried back to the couch. "I'll meet you outside, Mr. Blaine," he said. "Taz, go with him."

When they were gone, he took out the tape and scribbled a note to Lana on the pad beside the phone, telling her to listen to Delany's message, protect the tape, and wait for him to contact her. No answering machine. He wanted the line open in case Delany tried again.

Not a word about Taylor Blaine.

Then he whispered, "Hang on, Sloan, hang on."

Blaine was on the porch, hands in pockets, while Taz moved his Jeep to the street.

"Who's in the car?" Proctor asked.

"My son."

"I spoke to him on the phone."

Blaine nodded. "At my insistence, yes."

"He doesn't want me involved."

"No. He doesn't." The meaning was clear: *I'm still in charge.*

"Is he going with us?"

The limousine backed out, and the Jeep took its place. Proctor started down the side stairs, Blaine trailing.

"No, Mr. Proctor, he is not."

No chauffeur stepped out to open the door; Blaine did the honors himself, ushering Taz in first, then Proctor, who paused before he got in.

He intended to make it clear, now, that this was in no way a guarantee that he would take the old man's case. It was a fortuitous opportunity, nothing more, and nothing more should be construed from his acceptance of it.

"Time," Blaine said, tapping a wrist where his watch was hidden. "Time, Mr. Proctor."

He saw Blaine's eyes, then, and the pain.

The same pain he had seen in his own eyes, in the mirror, after he had heard Delany's voice.

for the love of God don't

Proctor nodded.

NINE

Flower Power felt like a slob.

She had had less than an hour from the time the phone rang to pack everything up and get out of town. No time for a shower, no time to do any laundry, no time for anything except pay her bill and split.

Leaving Crockston at the beginning of what probably would have been a profitable weekend was hardly her idea of a sound business decision. Still, she was in no position to push it, and besides, there was always next year.

The problem was, it was an election year, and election years are always hell on those fringe entertainment businesses where, if you believed every preacher in the Bible Belt, sin, corruption, and degradation flourished.

Places like the Kat Kave, for example, where she had once again worked most of the summer. Nicer than many strip clubs she had been in, with a bouncer the size of a mountain behind the bar and patrons who seldom, if ever, tucked less than a ten into her G-string. Of course it wasn't as classy as the high-price, neon-splashed clubs in Knoxville or

Nashville, Atlanta or Columbus, but she was realistic enough to know that women her age still playing a young woman's game had to pick and choose their spots.

Crockston was damn near perfect.

It had no university or college population to draw from for younger, firmer dancers; it had little competition from neighboring towns because, for the most part, there weren't any; and it was just isolated enough that someone like her, an out-of-towner, would be the major attraction.

It was definitely ideal.

Except when the sheriff was up for reelection in three weeks and had to go through the motions of cleaning the town up to protect the morals of the children and the sensibilities of the old biddies who smelled like talcum powder and dead lavender.

It was nice that the sheriff was a friend. He would call her motel room, say "Raids tonight, Flower, move your sorry ass, see you in the spring," and she would be gone.

Still, the least the sweet son of a bitch could have done was wait until Sunday. Four, five hundred dollars in lost revenue she would never recover.

She laughed, and glanced in the rearview mirror. Crockston had already slipped around the bend, leaving nothing but trees, the river, and a few lonely houses. Not a metropolis, that's for sure. Yet she kind of liked it here, truth be told. Far as she could tell, it lived on a pitifully small coal mine, a handful of tobacco farms, and a whole lot of campers, hikers, and lost tourists.

She felt a little sad, thought of the lost money, and laughed again.

What the hell; she still had her health, some decent looks for a dancer who had snuck past forty without telling a soul, and her silver box Mercedes. Not one of them fancy new ones all streamlined and boring; an old-fashioned, square-edged, built-like-a-truck sedan whose odometer had long ago given up counting the miles.

It coasted her along the highway beside the river, hardly making a sound, its unscratched hood reflecting the high clouds that had moved in just after dawn. No rain yet, but she reckoned that would hit long before she reached Tennessee.

She shivered a little and turned up the heat.

She didn't like the rain. It depressed her. It took away the sun and made her look older.

A campground on the left. She looked automatically and saw a couple of cars parked at the office. Fools, she thought; don't they know how cold it gets at night around here?

A mile farther along, and she passed the Cumberland Motel, no cars at all. That thing had been here since she'd first starting coming, maybe what? eight, nine years? She had no idea how it survived, and didn't particularly give a damn. She had met the owner in the market one afternoon, Sheriff Nathan had introduced them, and the look the woman had given her was one she had seen a million times before—*Jesus, don't touch me you disgusting little slut.*

Every year since then, Flower had hoped the place would burn down, with the smug little bitch still inside.

Not long afterward, before she was ready, she reached the tunnel.

She hated the tunnel.

Some guy once looked at that miserable excuse for a mountain and decided it would be easier to go through it, not around or over. Probably got off dynamiting holes in solid rock.

It was too dark in there.

No lights except what you could see at the far end almost half a mile away, and today, with the clouds, that wasn't much light at all.

She sped up, felt the car shimmy, and apologized to it silently.

When she reached the other side she realized she'd been holding her breath.

Her laugh, this time, had no humor in it at all.

She reached over to the passenger seat for her large straw purse, trying to fumble a pack of cigarettes out for her first of the day. Far ahead, on the right shoulder, she saw a dark lump and groaned aloud. Just what she needed—a poor deer hit by some jackass trucker or something. She hoped it was dead. One time she had passed one and could see its legs still twitching. She had gagged, nearly thrown up, crying the whole time.

She found the pack, braced her forearms against the steering wheel, took a cigarette out, and averted her gaze at the last second so she wouldn't see how badly the poor thing had been smashed up.

She was too late.

The pack and the cigarette slipped from her fingers, her hands strangled the wheel, and she said,

"Aw shit!" as she swerved onto the shoulder and stepped on the brakes.

It wasn't a deer.

It was a man.

And she thought she saw him move.

Taz felt like a slob.

After Proctor called, he had wasted no time trying to decide on a wardrobe. Simple shirt, jeans, leather jacket for the trip; his only suit and two more shirts for the fold-over garment bag he'd been ordered to buy when he had first taken the job. He had been halfway out the door before he realized that sneakers weren't going to cut it if he had to wear the suit, and had to run back for his only pair of good shoes. Maria hadn't helped, either, sitting naked on the bed, pouting, angry, loudly demanding explanations he didn't have. He had blown her a kiss, an apology, and he was gone.

A slob.

Sitting in a private plane that looked like the Presidential suite in some fancy hotel and he was wearing jeans, for crying out loud.

If his mother ever found out, she would kill him.

Blaine, on the other hand, didn't seem to mind.

"Are you comfortable, Mr. Tazaretti?"

"Yes, sir," he said. "Thank you."

He volunteered nothing more. That wasn't his job.

But he wasn't lying about the plane. The twelve seats were soft leather, large enough to be armchairs, and as he had inadvertently discovered, they swiveled at the base. They were spaced throughout the large cabin in such a way that conversations, if necessary, could be relatively private. In the back was a full-service galley, a small bedroom, two toilets, and a shower.

It had taken most of what he had not to gape, and the rest of it not to ask questions. That wasn't his job, either.

His job was to listen.

And watch.

In the limousine that had been easy. No one had said much of anything. The younger guy, Blaine's son, spent the whole time staring out the window as they sped toward Teterboro Airport as if the morning rush didn't exist. He probably thought he was being poker-faced or something, but it was clear he was royally pissed at his old man, turning his head only when Mr. Blaine picked up the phone and called the airport, making sure the plane was ready to go as soon as they arrived.

They had stared at each other then, and Taz had smiled politely. Franklin Blaine just looked away, back at the traffic.

And that, Taz had decided, is where the trouble's going to be if Proctor takes the old man's case. Whatever it is.

He didn't much care; he was too worried about Delany.

They were at the airport in less than half an hour; fifteen minutes later they were in the air.

They sat midway along in the main cabin with all but two of the stiff shades pulled down, the lighting dim; they made up three points of a loose triangle, a low rippled-slate, brass-rimmed table between them with indentations for cups and tumblers. Proctor was on his right, Blaine on his left, suit jacket open, tie undone and draped over the back of his seat.

He smiled at Taz. "I hate these things," he said, stabbing a thumb at the tie. "The older I get, the more I feel like I'm wearing a noose." When Taz couldn't help a glance at his jeans, the man added, "One of these days I'm going to chuck it all and wear dungarees and flannel shirts all damn day, the hell with the stockholders." And he laughed, loudly, heartily. "Well, that sure shows my age, doesn't it? Dungarees."

Taz grinned, laughed a little, but still felt uncomfortable.

And Proctor, by the look of him, probably wanted nothing more right now than to take over the cockpit and fly this thing south as fast as it would go.

Taz felt the same way.

It wasn't so much that he liked Delany any more or less than he liked the others, but Delany was Proctor's friend, he was part of Black Oak, and that was all he needed to fuel the urgency he felt.

Besides, there had been that voice . . . that scream.

The jet shimmied slightly.

Without thinking he gripped the armrests tightly, glanced out the port at his left shoulder, and looked away quickly. Trees and hills down there, nothing but trees and hills.

"Heights bother you, Mr. Tazaretti?" Blaine asked, not unkindly.

"Yeah," he answered with a sickly grin. "Planes, anyway."

Blaine nodded sympathetically, then suggested

that perhaps breakfast would help take his mind off the flight. A press of a button on his own armrest, and Taz heard movement behind him, saw Proctor straighten.

"This, gentlemen," said Blaine mildly, "is Chambers."

Taz couldn't help it this time.

He gaped.

Proctor saw Taz's reaction and immediately averted his gaze before he laughed aloud. He concentrated instead on the tray placed on the table—fried eggs, toast, orange juice in real glasses, jam, crisp bacon, home fries, a silver teapot, a silver coffeepot, real silverware, and a smoked-glass carafe of milk. Chambers handed each of them a china plate and suggested they begin before the food turned cold.

Then she took the seat between him and Taz, turned it around, and with a polite smile served herself.

"Vivian," Blaine explained as he waited his turn, "is a member of what you might call my inner circle. She has been with me for quite a while now, and"— he looked at Proctor—"I trust her completely."

Proctor only nodded.

"I have asked her here to help me plead my case."

Light brown hair with occasional winks of something lighter, something darker; slender in her business suit, sans tie, sans frills; a face with makeup that didn't try to hide the faint spray of freckles that spread from cheek to cheek; no jewelry save for a tiny pearl pendant at her open collar where a tie's knot would have been.

Blaine checked his watch. "We don't have much time, gentlemen, so forgive me if I don't wait until we've finished eating."

"Just so you know," Proctor reminded him.

Blaine nodded. "Of course. No guarantees. I understand that completely. If you turn me down, there will be no ill will here, no recriminations. All you have to do is listen, Mr. Proctor. All you have to do is listen."

Proctor believed him.

"Vivian, is everything ready on the ground?"

"Yes, Mr. Blaine. There'll be a car, no driver, at Roanoke. The route to Crockston will be marked on a map in the glove box. I think it will take less than three hours, because the roads are interstates until you get into Kentucky. After that, it's a two-lane county highway. I have no idea what's on it—gas stations, diners, motels, things like that—but Crockston itself is large enough to have just about everything you'll need. It does have an airport, but too small for us. Pleasure craft, mostly, and not very many of those. And there's too much fog there, nothing in or out anyway."

"Excellent," Blaine said.

"Thank you," Proctor said to her.

"It's my job, Mr. Proctor. No thanks are required."

The jet shimmied again.

Taz closed his eyes briefly and stopped chewing. When he reached for a cup of coffee, Proctor saw his hand shaking, just a little, just enough, and he couldn't help wondering if the kid was right for the job. This job.

Taz smiled at him.

Proctor wasn't reassured.

Flower could not release her grip on the steering wheel, nor could she bring herself to check the mirror to see if she had been right. One part of her was screaming for her to put the pedal down and leave nothing but smoke and tire tracks behind, this was none of her business, and did she really think, with her reputation, that she wasn't going to spend a few nights in a cell?; while another part, just as loud, wanted her to grab the damn cell phone she had spent so damn much money on and call Sheriff Nathan.

The phone was in her purse; the purse had fallen into the well beneath the dashboard.

She had to move in order to get it.

She had to move in order to drive away.

She braced herself and dared a look in the mirror.

Dead or dying, she couldn't tell.

All she could see was the blood.

TEN

I came back from the War, Blaine began without preface, then looked to Taz and raised an apologetic hand. The Second World War, young man, forgive me. For many of us, that is *the* War. I had lied about my age when I joined up, as many of us did, and I wish I could say I had been a hero, or that I even partook of some of the great battles. I did not. At least, not directly. For reasons best known to the gods that watch over me, I eventually found myself in England, then France, in Supply.

We were shot at, of course, and bombed a few times, but it was nothing compared to what others suffered.

And call me a coward or not, I did not volunteer to go forward.

As it turned out, I was pretty good at what I did, finding needed things. Scrounging, as it were. And finding people to do things that needed getting done, matching the skill with the job, if you see what I mean.

So when I returned at war's end, I looked around for something to do, something my newfound skills could capitalize on. It wasn't glamorous, but I chose contracting. My father was a carpenter, you see, and my uncle a plumber, and so I already knew something about building. And thanks to the army, I also knew something about how to get the materials I needed.

That was a good thing in those post-War boom times, because materials were often in short supply. GIs returning home, getting married, raising families . . . so I built houses. I took on a partner, Ben Hogan—no relation to the golfer, by the way— and *Hogan and Blaine* was born. With Ben along we built office buildings, too. Nothing fancy. Nothing very large. But by God, gentlemen, we built a lot of them. Actually, I built anything I could get a contract for. And if I didn't know how, I learned.

Time passed, and we grew.

I am not ashamed to say we also grew very wealthy, Ben and I.

Then, quite suddenly, he decided to bow out, go fishing at the ripe old age of forty. We did not argue, and there was no battle for supremacy within the company. He had had enough, and he called it quits, just like that.

It wasn't the same after he left, it wasn't as much fun. I diversified, as they say today, got into other things. The new stuff—electronics and such. Two years later I reached thirty-six and . . . I married my Iris.

He gazed out the window and was silent for a long time.

I blather sometimes, he continued, still watching the landscape and the clouds. Franklin and Alicia hate that. They think it's an imminent sign the old man's going nuts.

But they don't have as many memories as I.

One year after Iris and I married, in 1964, the first of our family was born. Franklin and Alicia. Twins; beautiful, precocious, adorable twins. Two years after that, Celeste was born. She was a difficult child, sickly for a while, and for a while we were afraid we would lose her. Thank God, we didn't. But she was never as smart as her brother and sister. She had to work hard for her grades, harder to be accepted by children her own age. Willful, you might say.

I think, more than the others, that she took after her father.

Do not misunderstand me. I could not have enjoyed my children more if they had been born when I was in my twenties, when most started families. Perhaps, because I was so much older than the norm for the time, I appreciated them more. I don't know. I don't care.

I am seventy years old, gentleman.

When I was fifty-seven . . . when I was fifty-seven . . .

"Taylor," said Vivian softly.

He shook his head—*I'm all right, please don't fuss*—and put a finger to one of the creases in his cheek.

Proctor couldn't see his face; he didn't have to.

We were in Connecticut. The family home. It was late June. Celeste had just turned eighteen. Nineteen eighty-four, it was. She was to attend Wellesley that fall, and was going to travel a little with two of her friends before locking herself away behind ivy-covered walls. We had been joking about George Orwell and such, because of the year. She was afraid Big Brother would take over sooner or later. I was of the opinion he already had.

I stood on the front porch and watched the three of them drive away. They were laughing, Mr. Proctor, waving out the windows and laughing.

She called her mother every other night for the next two weeks.

Every other night, Mr. Proctor, but I never saw her again.

Two years later, my Iris passed away. A massive stroke in the middle of the night. I am convinced it was the pressure of not knowing.

Whatever the reason, they're both gone now.

One, I have lost forever.

I want the other one back.

Blaine cupped his chin in his hand and stared at the sky. Proctor had a feeling he was looking at ghosts.

A minute passed; another.

He looked a question at Vivian, but she put a finger to her lips, shook her head, and gathered the breakfast dishes onto their tray. When Taz half rose, offering to help, she smiled him back into his seat and took everything back to the galley.

A soft chime sounded.

The jet shifted, banking slightly.

Vivian returned and stood behind her employer. "Mr. Blaine?" Her voice was soft; gentle. "Mr. Blaine, we'll be landing soon. Fifteen minutes." She paused. "Your seat, sir."

His chest expanded and he stared at the ceiling, then reached down and pressed a button on the side of his chair. It swiveled around to face front, and Proctor heard it lock into place as the old man fastened his seat belt. After some minor fumbling, he and Taz did the same; Vivian sat across the aisle.

Thirteen years, he thought; how can he expect anyone to find her after thirteen years?

Vivian reached across the narrow aisle to touch his arm, get his attention. Keeping her voice low, she said, "There's a guesthouse on the estate in Connecticut. I've lost count of how many file cabinets it has, and how many folders they hold."

"Reports," he guessed, his own voice low as well.

"Yes. State and local police, private investigators, psychics, mediums, tips from reward notices, forensic experts, the FBI—" She grinned at his startled look. "Mr. Blaine has friends in places you wouldn't believe, Mr. Proctor."

He glanced at the old man still staring out the window. "No," he said. "Actually, I don't think so." He didn't check on Taz. He suspected the kid was holding on for dear life, even though they were still a long way from the airport.

"She's not dead," Blaine said suddenly, forcefully. He turned his head toward Proctor; all the edges were hard. "She is not dead, and I will not die until I have found her."

The pain was still there, this time ringed with anger.

"She was taken, Mr. Proctor."

Proctor cleared his throat carefully. "Mr. Blaine, kidnapping is—"

"I said nothing about a kidnapping," Blaine snapped. "I have become a goddamn expert on kidnapping, and this wasn't one. I said she was taken."

For the first time since takeoff, Proctor heard the engines working, their pitch rising and falling as the plane lost altitude and angled for its approach.

"UFOs?" Taz blurted in disbelief.

Proctor could have strangled him.

Blaine, however, only lifted a hand. "UFOs. Government conspiracies. International terrorists. International conspiracy leaders. I dismiss none of it, gentlemen. Everyone else does, but I do not."

"You believe in Martians?" Taz asked incredulously.

Proctor snapped around to glare, but Taz was far too enthralled to pay attention.

The old man took a moment before he said: "I believe, Mr. Tazaretti, that only the supremely arrogant can dismiss out of hand the notion that we are, in this entire endless universe, alone." Suddenly he chuckled. "Martians, however, are extremely unlikely."

"Wow," Taz whispered. "Holy sh—cow."

Proctor sighed silently and faced front again. On top of Delany, this was too much. A guesthouse full of reports? From probably hundreds, maybe thousands, of experts? From the, can you believe it, FBI? Thirteen years and not one single clue?

And the old man doesn't dismiss the possibility of alien abduction?

For some kind of explanation, any kind would do, he looked to Vivian, who kept her face carefully, deliberately, maddeningly neutral. Not a twitch any-where—eyes, lips, or hands.

The chime sounded again, and he heard Taz shift.

Great, he thought; now he shuts up.

"Here is the deal," Blaine said.

Proctor didn't want to look at him, because any sign of encouragement would be a huge mistake, but he did. He couldn't avoid it.

"It's very simple, Mr. Proctor, don't look so appre-hensive. You will allow me to hire Black Oak—which means you, sir—to find out what happened to my daughter. I will pay all your expenses, I will give you access to every one of my contacts as they become necessary, I will give you the run of my house, my offices wherever they may be, and my staff. I will give you free rein to do whatever you want, what-ever it takes.

"In addition, I will pay you enough above and beyond so that you will never have to work on any-thing else in your life."

He held out his hand.

Proctor didn't take it.

"You refuse?" Blaine said, neither surprised nor insulted.

"If I accept," Proctor told him, "I will run my busi-ness as usual. I have clients, sir, who depend on me and my people. And frankly, this case is so old . . . the odds against the results you're looking for are great."

"Great," Blaine echoed mockingly. "What you mean is, a hell of a hell of a hell of a hell of a long shot. Slim to none, and slim is out of the question."

"Yes, sir, that is exactly what I mean."

Blaine's hand didn't retreat.

"And you have to work," he said thoughtfully. "Other cases, that is. My . . . my daughter will be just one among many."

Proctor nodded. "Yes, I do have to work. I'd go nuts if I didn't. Even with all those reports and contacts and whatever of yours, there's going to be a lot of downtime. Time when I'll be just twiddling my thumbs, as it were. I can't live like that. Your own story tells me you can't either. Which tells me you don't like it, but you do understand."

Blaine returned his gaze steadily.

For the first time, Proctor looked at the hand, then looked up. "But your daughter will *not* be just one case among many. None of my cases are, Mr. Blaine. None."

A third chime.

Vivian whispered, "Almost down."

Blaine finally looked away, but his hand did not move.

"There are hundreds of other agencies," Proctor said.

"No," Blaine said. "No, there are not."

Taz moaned softly.

Blaine smiled. "Is that a comment on my pilot, or on the deal you're not accepting?"

Proctor couldn't help it; he smiled back. "On his mortality, I think."

The plane touched the runway with a faint lurch and squeal, both men were eased forward when the engines reversed and the brakes were applied, and Proctor, without thinking, took the old man's hand.

Blaine's smile broadened; his grip was snug without testing.

"You won't regret this, Ethan," he said.

"It's Proctor," Proctor said. "Nobody calls me Ethan. And yeah, sure I'm going to regret this. You and I, we're going to fight like cats and dogs."

Blaine laughed. "Very good . . . Proctor. And you're right. We will. Often." He laughed again. "It keeps me young."

Proctor said nothing. He was too busy trying to figure out what he had just done, why he had done it, and how he was going to explain it to Lana and Doc. By the time he gave up, the plane had taxied to a halt near a small hangar, and Taz was on his feet, bag in hand, ready to leave.

Vivian opened the forward hatch and gestured. "The stairs are ready. You can—" She looked out and frowned.

Proctor watched her uneasily as he unbuckled his seat belt.

He heard footsteps on metal, saw her reach out and say something to someone outside. When she turned around, her neutral expression had slipped just a little.

"Mr. Proctor," she said. "There's a policeman out here. He has a message for you."

ELEVEN

The mist wasn't heavy, but it was enough to keep the windshield wipers moving slowly. Scraps of clouds hung high on the thickly wooded mountains. Autumn colors were dulled, except when an infrequent break in the overcast let the sun touch part of a slope; then it was as if a torch had been lit.

Proctor drove without speaking.

Taz didn't mind. He didn't feel much like talking himself. A word of direction once in a while, that was all. A glance at the map Vivian Chambers had handed him, a check of the exits along I-81 that would direct them into Kentucky . . . and a word now and then.

This wasn't what he had signed on for.

Nobody died in the scams he looked into. A fistfight now and then, maybe somebody blows his stack and goes after someone else with a pipe or a bat, there's a lot of yelling, punches thrown, dancing around and taunting. A bruise, a black eye.

But nobody died.

This was absolutely not what he had signed on for.

The cop who had met the plane was a state trooper, and how he had gotten the word or knew how to deliver it to Blaine, Taz didn't know. Over the past couple of hours he had vacillated between desperately wanting to know how it was done, and equally desperately not wanting to know any such thing. It was like the Brooklyn neighborhood his cousin Danny lived in—things happened, good and not so good, and it was worth your life to ask who and how and why.

It happened.

You accepted it.

You went on with your life.

All Proctor had said was, "Thank you, Officer," thanked Blaine and the woman, and walked directly to the car waiting for them on the tarmac. Taz had followed silently with a last minute over-the-shoulder see-you-later wave to the old man in the hatchway. Taz hadn't offered to drive because, from the look on Proctor's face, he figured he would rather keep his head on his shoulders, where it belonged.

"Navigate," was all his boss had said after that.

He did, while he watched the late-morning sun get sucked in by the clouds that thickened the farther west they drove.

When the mist finally began, he had to remind Proctor to turn on the wipers. When the mist wouldn't let up, he had to remind Proctor not to drive so fast, there were slicks on the interstate, rooster-tail sprays from the eighteen-wheelers, and nuts who thought a damp road was as safe as a dry one.

Proctor had obeyed with a formal "I'll remember, Taz," and nothing more.

Finally, just as they passed a faded "Welcome to

Kentucky" sign, Taz leaned his head back and said, "Well . . . shit," to the ceiling.

Proctor grunted.

Five minutes later he said, "I liked him"; the best epitaph he could say.

"So did I, Taz," Proctor said. "So did I."

Thirty miles later they left the interstate for a narrow highway that hugged the east bank of a river that didn't know the meaning of the word straight. Proctor was forced to slow down; it was clear he didn't like it very much.

Finally Taz twisted around until he leaned against the door and looked at his boss. "I . . ." He sniffed, rubbed a hand across the back of his neck, and looked through the windshield. "The night I had to look at that picture."

Proctor glanced over.

"I came up with the damnedest thing, you know?" He smiled to himself. "Space vampire. You believe it? A space vampire." He inhaled slowly. "Lana, maybe it was Doc, reminded me I had forgotten something." He looked at Proctor again. "Consider the source, they said." He shrugged with one shoulder. "Delany was the source. That's when I knew."

Proctor switched on the headlamps. In some states, now, it was the law, whenever it rained. The mist in spots had become more like fog, and the beams turned pale and weak.

"The thing is," he said. Paused. Rubbed his neck a second time because he knew he was putting it square on the block. "I mean, they said he was hit by a car, boss." He shook his head and pointed at the road. "How? Here? What cars?"

"We're not there yet," Proctor said, but he tilted his head. Waiting.

"No offense, and I liked him, I already told you that, but what was he doing walking out there? Delany? On a highway? He only walked from the door to the bar. Unless it was for one of those godawful things he wanted to buy." Encouraged that Proctor hadn't snapped his head off, he straightened. "Now the source here is the state police, right? And I guess they got the word from the local police, or somebody local, from around where he was staying."

He stopped when he saw a doe and her fawn on the side of the road. *Wow,* he said silently, turning around to watch them as long as he could; *Wow.*

"Taz," Proctor prodded gently.

"Oh." He faced front and prayed he wasn't blushing. "Yeah. Sorry. It's . . . I mean, that wasn't any car I heard on the answering machine, Proctor."

"Okay."

"So who are they kidding?"

A car came at them in the other lane, slipping out of the mist, slipping away. It was the first vehicle Taz had seen since leaving the interstate.

"They don't know about the tape," Proctor said.

"Maybe."

"They don't."

"But—"

"Taz." Proctor smiled; it was quick, but it was a smile. "They said he had been hit by a car. They did not say they had pulled him out of the wreck of a roadside telephone booth. "You," and he pointed, "are you jumping to conclusions."

"Look," Taz said, frustrated, "what I'm saying is—"

"What you're saying is . . . Delany may have been murdered."

He opened his mouth, closed it, and blinked. Jesus, he thought; I am, ain't I?

He considered it for a while, wanting to make sure he had it all straight in his head. This was the first time he had been in the field, as Doc always put it, with the boss, and the one thing he didn't want to do was look like an idiot.

He didn't want Proctor to be sorry he was along.

Then he said, "Hey, look."

A sign on the right that looked as if it were being slowly eaten by trees: CUMBERLAND MOTEL AND MUSEUM OF THE ODD. 5 MILES.

"You think maybe . . . ?"

He waved his hand sharply in dismissal. There was no need to answer. If Delany had gotten this far, he wouldn't have passed up a place like that. No way in hell.

The car hummed over a bridge, and Taz looked down at the broad stream that fed into the river just beyond. The water moved swiftly, white where it rolled over submerged rocks. Rocky banks, and trees that hugged the water. He had never seen so damn many trees in his life. If anybody lived around here, you wouldn't know until all the leaves had fallen.

He eased the window down with a button on the center console and listened to the snake-hiss of the tires, squinted at the blur of trees; it didn't take him long to realize that the tires were the only thing he could hear. No traffic, horns, brakes, sidewalk music . . . nothing.

It spooked him into closing the window again.

They passed through a long unlit tunnel, and he had a childish urge to lean over and honk the horn.

He saw Proctor's hand move then, a twitch for the horn instantly corrected, and he grinned.

Then he said, "Okay, so what are we going to do?"

What Proctor wanted to do was find the nearest bus or train station and send the kid home where he belonged.

What he wanted to do was get a neck in his hands, any neck, and squeeze.

What he wanted to do was pull over, get out, and find something to hit. Anything. If it hit back, so much the better.

Because he couldn't, there was acid in his stomach, and tension in his arms and neck, and too many unanswered questions for him to think very clearly.

He drove on, grateful that Taz at least had the sense to hold his tongue. At the same time, he wished the kid would talk. Say something. Anything. Just to keep the car full of noise, so he wouldn't keep listening to the last sound Delany made.

"There," Taz said.

He looked over and saw the Cumberland Motel, at least five cabins that he could count before the site was gone. It didn't look like much, but it was a place to check out. Taz was right; Delany wouldn't have passed this up for the world.

"Have you been watching?" he finally asked.

Taz nodded. "Nothing."

"I know."

"Not even a dead flare, you know? I thought they always put down flares or something, to warn the traffic. Haven't seen a telephone either."

"Maybe we haven't reached it yet."

Although the clouds remained, the mist stopped and the sky brightened. There wasn't much land between the highway and the river—the shoulder, a few yards of dirt and trees and bushes, and a fairly sharp drop to the water. On the other side, the slopes were easy, wooded, without much underbrush at all.

Eventually there were dirt roads marked with mailboxes; eventually there were clearings with houses near the back; eventually the slopes backed away.

Then Taz said with a grin, "Well, okay."

On the left was a long, low, brick building with a single door in front, surrounded by a paved parking lot. A neon sign on the peaked roof announced the Kat Kave. A sign at the parking-lot entrance announced Flower Power as the main attraction. A wide, empty, brush-choked lot separated it from a twelve-unit, two-story motel.

"Flower Power?" Taz said.

Proctor shrugged. "Before your time."

A hundred yards farther on, the houses began, and Taz said in singsong, "We're here."

The mountain had stopped as if sliced off, and in the gap between it and the next rise, was Crockston proper.

Regular streets now, all ending at the highway. The houses became businesses, with canvas awnings and the occasional sidewalk bench. There wasn't a single tree along the main road, just poles and sidewalks. Road signs pointed the way to West Virginia, to Lexington; universal travel signs for a hospital and an airport. Midway along, a narrow bridge crossed the river to a broad flatland of homes. On a far slope to the north twin smokestacks streamed white toward the clouds. On telephone poles were handmade signs for garage sales, professional signs for an upcoming election.

Few parking spaces were taken, few pedestrians, and less traffic.

Cloud cover and surrounding mountains seemed to squeeze everything into a smaller space, and Proctor couldn't shake the feeling that Crockston wasn't nestled in the Cumberlands, it huddled.

"First," he decided, "we'll find a place to stay. Then—"

Taz pointed over his shoulder. "Well, what about—"

"Forget it," he said with a smile.

"Just thought I'd mention it."

"Sure." He stopped at a red light. "Look for a hotel."

"Ha."

"Okay, a motel that doesn't look too bad."

"What about the cops?"

"Taz, you have to remember one thing: we have no official capacity at all. We're private, and I don't know anyone around here. We set up a base, we go meet the local chief or sheriff, and we hope he'll be cooperative."

"Then what?"

The light changed.

"Then we find out what happened to Delany."

It didn't take long to reach the other end of town. Proctor pulled into a driveway to make a U-turn, and headed back. The police station and fire department were two blocks away, part of the same brick building. Almost new, as was the town hall a block later. Too new, Proctor thought; they didn't look as if they belonged.

When they reached the bridge again, he stopped for another light.

Taz said, not too disappointed, "I think we're out of luck. I didn't see anything."

Proctor hadn't either, which meant they would either have to hunt for a bed-and-breakfast, which in this town was doubtful, or go back. Not to the motel by the strip club, however. He didn't think Taz could take the strain.

"Looks like we'll have to do that Cumberland place."

Proctor looked at him. "Good boy."

Taz made a face. "Thanks. I guess. Besides," he added, "how bad can it be?"

TWELVE

Just as the bridge light changed, Taz announced that he was hungry, and Proctor was startled to realize that he was too. Although the breakfast on Blaine's jet had been substantial, he had tasted little of it, and the mention of food now made his stomach growl. He turned left, drove up the street until he could turn around, and returned to the highway. On the corner of the police-station block he had seen the Blue Sky Diner, and as long as they were there, they might be able to make their first contact as well. The motel could wait.

The diner's parking lot was on the side street behind the stucco-sided building, with only a pair of pickups and an old Mercedes Proctor looked at with envy as he climbed out. Not bad, he thought as he walked around it; no rust that he could see, the tires were new, and the inside was clean. Two suitcases and a jumble of old and new college textbooks on the backseat; Tennessee plates.

"God, that thing is old," Taz said, waiting impatiently, slipping sunglasses on.

Proctor shook his head and led him around the building to the corner entrance. No surprise—a counter on the left, window booths on the right all the way to the back.

What was a surprise was the silence.

Two men in working clothes sat at the counter, eating without looking up; a woman in the fourth booth stared unhappily out her window; behind the counter, a waitress leaned against the serving gap shelf and watched someone in the kitchen.

No music, no scrape of utensils, not even someone clearing a throat.

None of them looked up when he led the way to the last booth.

Once down, he shed his sport coat and closed his eyes with a sigh. When Taz took his seat, he opened his eyes, blinked, and pointed at the kids's sunglasses, gesturing to take them off. With that long black hair and black-leather jacket, Taz couldn't have looked more like a fifties hood if he tried. In a place like this that was no compliment or recommendation.

The window at his left shoulder overlooked the side street. Still not much traffic, pedestrian or otherwise. That surprised Proctor. It was lunch hour, but not many people seemed to be taking advantage.

Crockston seemed small, but it couldn't be that small.

The waitress took their order, raising a well-penciled eyebrow at the list Taz gave her, shrugging at Proctor with a weary automatic smile—*the kid must have hollow legs*—and returned to her station behind the counter, moving only when one of the men lifted his cup for more coffee.

"Howdy, stranger," he whispered. "New in town? Just passing through?"

"What?" Taz said.

Proctor waved him off. It was the suddenness of the trip, his lack of decent sleep, and concern about Delany. He was, in a sense, seeing things that weren't there.

Taz checked the window, checked the counter and the other booths, pulled a packet of sweetener from a cup and toyed with it, spinning it between thumb and forefinger, forward, then backward. "Now what?"

"Now," Proctor said calmly, "we eat. Or I will, at least, because I'm going to kill you if you don't knock it off."

Taz frowned, looked at his fingers, and quickly pushed the packet away, clasping his hands and resting them on the table. "Sorry."

"Don't worry about it."

Taz glanced around the room again, and leaned over the table. "It's just that . . . I don't know, but . . ." He exhaled sharply. "Does this place seem right to you?"

Proctor settled back, uncertain he'd heard right. "What do you mean?"

The kid jerked a thumb at the window and the street beyond. "Okay. It's like . . . I don't know. It's like there aren't any people here, you know that I mean? I mean, jeez, boss, it's lunchtime, we're right next to a cop shop, and there are only five people in here counting you and me." He leaned back and picked up the sweetener again. "Wasn't much traffic, either, in case you didn't notice."

"A lousy day. People tend to stay home."

"It isn't raining. It isn't windy. It isn't that cold."

Proctor did his best not to smile, pleased at the kid's reaction; the same as his own. "So . . . what do you figure?"

"I don't know. I just know it's not right. I mean, it doesn't feel right."

Proctor watched the waitress hip through the swinging doors that led to the kitchen, a large tray in her hands. He held up a finger—*hold that thought*—and smiled at her as she spread the lunch across the table.

She didn't smile back.

When she was finished, she grumbled, "You need something, I'm over there, don't have to holler, I ain't deaf," and walked stiffly away.

Taz watched her as well, looked at the hamburger platter in front of him, and picked up a french fry. Tested it, and nodded his opinion. "And what," he grumbled as he chewed, "about all that Southern hospitality I've always heard about?"

"Well, son," a voice said, "some days you just don't feel like getting up in the morning."

He was taller for the solid weight he carried in his chest and arms. Shirt and trousers were a matching grey, his open windbreaker dark, with police patches high on each arm. His Western hat had been white at some time, but weather and wearing had darkened it, softened it. Just like his face.

He stood with his hands clasped loosely in front of him, a hint of a smile on his lips while Taz choked on his fry, reddening with embarrassment and anger, ready to rise out of his seat, one hand in a fist.

"Don't bother," the man said mildly, pulling his

jacket to one side to expose a badge pinned to his breast pocket. "Just makes things messy." He smiled at Proctor, a professional smile, and when Taz had caught his breath, said, "Scoot on over, son," but didn't wait until he had. He nudged his way onto the seat, easing the plates over with one hand while the other took off his hat and hung it on one of the hooks at booth's end.

"Afternoon, Chief," Proctor said.

"Sheriff," the man corrected amiably. "Sheriff Corliss Nathan. Cory, to those who want to live long lives."

They shook hands while Taz wiped furiously at his mouth, smearing catsup across his chin. Proctor mimed wiping it off, and Taz glared at him.

"So," the sheriff said, plucking one of the fries off the plate. "You're here about the salesman, right?"

With a glance Proctor reminded Taz of his role, then shook his head. "He wasn't a salesman, Sheriff. He worked for me. He was on vacation."

"Ah." Another fry, this one dunked into the mound of catsup Taz had poured. "Well, I'm sorry for your loss. Really."

"What happened?" Proctor said, more a demand than a question.

"Hit-and-run," the sheriff answered matter-of-factly. "There are roads on both sides of the river, but this one's the best. Goes clear down to the interstate one way, the other way eventually goes clear over near to Lexington. We get people who look at a map, figure it's a shortcut to one place or another, then find out it ain't anything of the sort." He shrugged. "They go like bats out of hell, even through town. Spring and fall, deer drop like flies."

"My friend wasn't a deer."

"No. No, sir, he sure wasn't." He snagged another fry, and Taz, in disgust, shoved the plate over. "Thanks, son, appreciate it. Be on my tab."

"No problem," Taz muttered, then grabbed the remainder of his hamburger before the sheriff could take it.

Nathan grinned, raised a heavy eyebrow. "This man—Delany, right?—this man have family?"

"I'm afraid I'm it," Proctor answered. "All his people are gone."

"Doubly sorry for your loss, then."

Proctor almost smiled. The man was good, he had to give him that; he was really good.

"Thing is," the sheriff continued, taking another fry, "best I can figure, he was on the shoulder late last night, early this morning, probably this morning, for some reason or other; some half-looped jackass in a car or pickup barrels along, don't see him, and . . ." He had the grace to scowl and look away. "The sorry son of a bitch didn't stop, and didn't stop long enough to report it. Sorry to say, Mr. Proctor, your friend was long gone before we got to him."

Proctor forced himself to take a bite of his sandwich, a drink of his coffee. Cardboard and mud. "If it's okay with you, I'd like to see him."

"Well, thing is, I was gonna take you there anyway. Official identification and all. We have his papers, credit cards and such, but I assume you already know the routine, hard as it is."

Proctor nodded solemnly, noting from the corner

of his vision Taz staring out the window. Seeing nothing. Jaw working. Swallowing hard.

"How did you find him?"

The sheriff cocked an eyebrow. "Thought you'd never ask." He raised his left hand and crooked a finger. When nothing happened, he looked over his shoulder and beckoned. The woman in the third booth hesitated, then slid out.

Proctor's first thought was that a dead body was a hell of a thing for a woman to come across; his second nearly made him laugh aloud because it was more a Taz reaction: wow.

She wasn't more than an inch or two over five feet, her fair hair was cropped short, her face not quite lean, and light emerald eyes that concentrated on the floor. The baggy sweater and loose jeans, however, could not disguise the fact that she had a full figure. A very full figure. One that instantly turned male brains and political sensibilities into teenage mush.

He slid over with a welcoming nod to allow her to sit beside him. This close, he saw the ghost-lines her spare makeup couldn't quite hide. And something in the eyes he couldn't quite place.

She sat on the edge, hunched, head down, hands clenched in her lap. Her head barely reached his shoulder, even sitting, and she didn't look up.

"Gentlemen," Nathan said politely, "this here is Flower Power, the lady who found your friend."

Taz's head snapped around so fast, Proctor thought his neck would break, and he cautioned, "Taz," quickly before the kid could blurt what was clearly on his mind.

Flower's hands stayed in her lap, fingers tracing

knuckles. "I'm sorry," she said quietly, still staring at her hands. "There was nothing I could do."

"Now, Flower," Nathan said, "nobody's blaming you for anything, okay? You don't worry about it, hear?"

She nodded, but Proctor saw her shudder.

An awkward silence, before Taz, using a forefinger to wipe crumbs from his lips, said, "How'd you know it was us, Sheriff Nathan?"

The sheriff tilted his head back and studied the ceiling for a moment. "You know, that's a funny thing, Mr. Tazaretti. That right? Tazaretti? Funny thing. Thought all I had was a dumbass hit-and-run this morning getting me out of bed. Not unusual for that road, like I told you, but not rare enough for my peace of mind, if you know what I'm talking about. Anyway, I'm in the office, taking Flower's statement here, and I get a call from the state police. I had already reported it so's they could keep an eye out. For what, I don't know, but that's the rules." He sniffed, took a fry, dunked it in catsup, nibbled on it for a few seconds. "I figured they wanted to clarify something, or maybe tell me they already got the bastard. But instead, they tell me to expect somebody. I ask if it's family, they don't tell me squat." He looked at Proctor, not happy at all. "I don't like not knowing squat, Mr. Proctor. Makes me kind of nervous."

"We're not spies," Proctor responded evenly. "We're not reporters. And we're definitely not government."

"Got friends, though."

On another day, he might have answered *not really*.

Today, however, he only nodded a *you could say that*. But in such a way that he hoped the man wouldn't take offense.

"Well," the sheriff said, "your friend's lucky you got other friends. Ain't that right, Flower? If he ain't got family, he would've been buried here, town expense." His face hardened for a moment. "Hell of a way to end up, Potter's field halfway to nowhere."

Proctor offered some of his lunch to the woman, but she shook her head quickly. Almost as if he had threatened to strike her for the refusal. A glance to Taz, who immediately resumed looking out the window, and he said, "I run a security firm, Sheriff. Nothing big, nothing special. Taz here is one of my people. Sloan Delany worked for me too. I came down because . . ." He spread his hands. "He was a friend, a very good friend, and I want to know what happened." He paused, wishing they were having this conversation somewhere else. The sheriff, however, didn't seem inclined to move. "Delany isn't usually that careless."

The sheriff nodded. "A drinking man?"

"Not so much that he'd walk alone on a dark highway in the middle of the night."

Nathan rubbed the side of his nose thoughtfully, then tilted his head in a quick what-can-I-tell-you shrug.

One of the men at the counter dropped a bill by his cup and left; the other rapped his plate with a fork to get the waitress's attention.

No one else had come in.

"Tell you what," the sheriff said, wiping his hands on a napkin. "Why don't I take y'all over to the hospital now, that's where we've got the morgue, such as it is. You can do the formalities and such. Then, if you want, we can head on back to my office and you can check the reports."

Proctor accepted the offer gratefully and thanked him for the courtesy. "But I don't want you to think I'm checking up on you, Sheriff." He tapped, then rubbed his temple. "My own peace of mind."

"No problem, Mr. Proctor. Glad to do it. If your friend was like you said, I'd kind of like to know myself what he was doing out there." He sighed in resignation. "Thing like this, though, I don't expect we'll ever know."

He raised a hand, and the waitress hurried over, ripping the check off her pad. "My tab, Verna," he said blithely, folding the paper and slipping it into his breast pocket. "Settle up with you later."

She muttered, "Sure you will," and left, poking her pencil back into her hair.

Proctor remembered Taz's comment about Southern hospitality, but it wasn't distrust he had seen on the woman's face; it was nerves. Just short of fear.

"Miss Power," he said then, a brief touch to her shoulder, "I want to thank you for what you did. Where I come from, sadly, a lot of people would have just driven on. Taz and I really appreciate it."

"Yeah," Taz said, his voice tight. "That's right, we do."

Sheriff Nathan slid out of the booth, a show of grunting and groaning and complaining about places too small for a man his size. He slapped on his hat, held a hand out for Flower, but she didn't move.

"Flower? Flower, honey, let's go."

She didn't move.

Proctor touched her again. "Miss Power, are you all right?"

She turned her head so fast, it took him a moment to focus because she was so close.

"There's something," she said.

"Now damnit, Flower," the sheriff said, reaching for her arm.

"Something," she repeated firmly, twisting away from his grip. "Something else."

THIRTEEN

Dewey Plowman was ready to get rich.

He had been ready for years, but an itchy palm and instinct told him this time was it.

And Grayleen would never turn him down again.

He sat under a tarp lean-to he had rigged at the back of a spit of land that extended into the river from the tunnel hill's outside slope. Brush and small trees on either side kept him hidden from the highway; across the way, nothing but more trees, more underbrush. He couldn't be more invisible than if he'd taken one of them formula drinks he seen on the TV.

Water dripped onto the tarp.

The river flowed dark and slow.

Wearing an open wool coat near the color of mud, jeans over long johns, and hiking boots, he sat on his sandwich bed—blanket, plastic, blanket; to keep his butt dry—and did his best not to bounce with impatience.

Not the best hunter in the world, but he'd still learned the value of not paying attention to time. If it came, it came, and he was ready; if it didn't, there was always tomorrow, or the next day, or the day after that. He'd still be ready.

Soon as he'd heard the word about the salesman that morning, he'd known.

Sheriff, of course, what else is new, was putting it out that it was a hit-and-run, and the driver was probably already three counties over by now. Maybe even up into West Virginia or over to the Commonwealth.

Crock.

It was a crock, and everyone knew it.

Half the guys going to work in other towns, riding down into the mine, were armed one way or another. Doors were locked; shades drawn; he wouldn't be surprised to learn half the school was missing today.

Not to worry, folks, he thought; it'll all be over soon.

Dewey Plowman didn't give a shit about saving the town.

Rich.

He was going to be rich.

At first he had considered going up on Spooner Mountain, knowing the trails the way he did, but he also knew that the folks who lived back there in the hollers, they weren't about to ask for identification before letting loose a round or two. Just his luck, he'd get plugged.

A sudden gust of wind rippled the tarp, spilling water over the edges, blurring his vision.

The sun faded again.

He lit a cigarette, and watched the smoke drift.

Every so often his left hand would glide along the old Remington's worn stock at his side. A reassurance. A comfort. Later he would bring it into his lap. For now, he would keep it where it was. It wasn't dark enough yet, but if he held it too soon—he knew himself too well—he'd end up blowing away every twig and leaf that made a noise behind him.

Tobacco smoke drifted.

The river moved on.

He didn't hear the footfall until it was too late.

The Kat Kave was much deeper than it appeared from the highway. The back exit opened onto a wide, overhang-covered wood porch where the bartenders and dancers would stand for a while or lean against the waist-high rail, for the peace, for the fresh air. The yard was five feet below and sloped downward in sparse grass and ruddy earth until it ended abruptly in trees and boulders that covered a steep slope. The only light was over the lintel, just bright enough to keep the shadows from getting too close.

Grayleen sat on the flat railing, facing the door, a patched cardigan caped over her shoulders. She was early, it was only about three, but it paid sometimes to come in like this, especially on weekends. Girls called in sick, girls quit without notice, and it all gave her extra time onstage. Extra time, extra bucks.

She straightened, and arched her back, eyes half-closed. Tonight she was a redhead, fire to match her lipstick, and she had a good feeling. A real good feeling. She smiled to herself and sagged a little for comfort. Of course payday at the mine always brought a good feeling. That's why she worked at this one step up from a dive, driving all the way in from Knott County to a place she wouldn't have lived in on a bet. Fresh money, eager faces, hands filled with bills ready to be tucked in all the right places.

Even better, that Power bitch had left, which meant she would be the main deal. Five hundred easy, maybe a little more if she wasn't too tired and the guy was cute and his wallet was full.

The iron fire door creaked open just wide enough for Helly to stick her head out.

"You got smokes?" she asked hopefully, squinting around as if expecting a mob to be waiting.

"No," Grayleen said wearily. "I didn't have them before, I don't have them now."

Helly made a face. "No call for nasty, honey. Just asking, that's all." She put one bare foot on the porch and shivered. "Damn, it's cold out here."

"You're half-naked, you stupid bitch, that's why," Grayleen said with a lopsided grin. She still had her shirt and jeans on; Helly was always in her gaudy cheap kimono, not a stitch on underneath. Two hours yet before the first set. The woman was a jerk.

"Charity says—"

Grayleen snorted. "Charity only wants to let her hands do the talking through the money you make her. You're not careful she'll try to set you with good ol' Wilford."

Helly giggled. "I could think of worse guys." She wrinkled her nose. "Your lover, Dewey, for starters."

Grayleen leaned over and swung a mock-slap that made Helly jerk back, laughing. "He is not my lover. There ain't enough money in the world put me on his mattress."

Helly, who still hadn't put on her eyebrows or lipstick, her thin face lightly pocked, came all the way out, taking the one step down as if she were moving onto thin ice. She was tall, the tallest in the Kave, but without, Grayleen thought, much of a figure to go with it. She hugged herself as she stared at the trees, still squinting.

Grayleen sighed loudly. "Girl, when are you going to get contacts, huh?"

Helly shrugged.

"Well, next time you fall off the damn stage, remember I warned you."

Helly's face reddened. "That was an accident. I was into the music, was all."

"Yeah, yeah, sure."

Droplets formed along the edge of the gutterless roof, catching the light, winking as they fell.

"You hear about Flower?"

Grayleen snorted. "She's gone, big deal."

Helly shook her head. "No." She looked around as if afraid someone was listening. "No, she found a body this morning."

"You're shitting me."

"No, really. On the road. Sheriff claims to was a hit-and-run." Her tone said, *but we know better.*

Grayleen covered her eyes with one hand. "Oh, great. That's just . . . great."

"Grayleen?"

Grayleen slid off the railing and swatted it angrily. "Do you believe it? I mean, do you just believe it? God damn, Helly, it's payday, you know? Payday!"

"Grayleen."

"I don't live right, you know? I just do not live right."

"Grayleen, damnit, there's someone in the trees."

*   *   *

"Goddamnit!" Dewey yelled as he scrambled out of the lean-to. "Goddamnit, you scared me half into next Thursday." Then he lunged back under to swipe his cigarette off the sandwich bed, burned his palm, and swore again.

Maggie Medford stuck her hands into her pockets and laughed. Her jeans were tucked into high, ridge-soled boots, and her camouflage jacket was a size too large and too long. Her hair was covered by a baseball cap.

"What the hell are you doing here anyway?" he demanded, one eye nearly shut in a suspicious squint.

She took in the lean-to and the Remington, and looked at him with a grin. "I could ask the same, Dewey." She glanced around the spit. "What're you up to?"

"Hunting," he said reluctantly.

"What, ducks? Geese?"

"Yeah. That."

She walked down to the water, looked upriver and shook her head slowly. He was tempted, really tempted, to shove her in, see if she could swim. But if she could, and she caught him . . . he backed off a step and waited.

It wasn't like she hadn't already figured it out.

She faced him, a touch of a breeze stirring her hair. Then she looked up at the road. "So you figure, that guy was found over there, right? You figure the criminal always returns to the scene of the crime."

At least she didn't laugh at him. Not out loud, anyway.

"Got my reasons, Maggie."

"Oh, I'm sure you do." She came toward him, not looking at him, checking out each bush she passed, once pinching off one last dead leaf. Then she held up a finger. "The thing is, Dewey, and pay attention here 'cause I'm only going to say it once, the thing is that what you're looking for don't exist." A mild look on her face that, to him, might as well have been a glare. "Every time somebody gets himself run over, every time some idiot shoots himself in an accident, falls over a cliff, trips on a deadfall, you and half the jerk-offs in this town got to get your manly weapons and head for the hills."

The finger jabbed his chest.

"It don't exist, Dewey."

Jab.

"You never saw it, I never saw it, Mr. John Wayne Sheriff Corliss Nathan never saw it."

Jab; a little harder.

He took another step back.

"Nobody has ever seen it, Dewey Plowman, and nobody ever will because the god damn . . . son of a bitching thing . . . does not exist."

The finger hooked around his lapel as if to draw him closer.

"Dewey. Honey. I don't know how to make it any clearer."

He stared at the ground, feeling like a ten-year-old taking a scolding from his mother. "What do you care what I do?" he muttered, and had to stop himself from toeing the ground.

"Because," she answered, lowering her voice, "you're a nice guy, Dewey. You help me out when

I need a strong back. Have ever since my Jack died."
She shoved him playfully. "So I care about you, you thickheaded rheumy. You sit out here in this kind of weather, you're going to get sick and then what'll I do, huh? Huh?"

He didn't know how to answer that because most of it was true. The helping-out stuff, anyway. She, however, could get along without him just fine. Handymen in this town were two dozen to the penny.

"Maggie—"

"No." She reached into the lean-to and picked up the rifle, hooked her arm around it, and took his elbow with her free hand. "It's going to rain soon. Any minute. And look at you, you're freezing!"

Chilly, he contradicted silently; I'm just a little chilly, that's all.

"Come on back to the motel. I'll fix you something warm before you head for the Kave."

"I do not go to the Kave, Maggie," he insisted self-righteously.

"Oh, sure, and I go to church three times a week." She laughed and tugged at his arm. "Move it, skunk, before I have to carry you."

There was no arguing with her when she was like this, so he went. After hurrying back to fetch his sandwich bed. Besides, she was right. About the rain, anyway. He could see circles in the water erased as they were formed. Pretty soon they'd be fountains, and the ground would turn to mud.

It never came out in the rain.

He was pretty sure of that.

It never came out in the rain.

He dumped the bed in the back of her pickup, and slumped in the passenger seat, hunched over, arms folded across his chest, just to let her know he wasn't no kid and didn't appreciate being treated like one.

She hummed tunelessly during the short drive back to the motel, shooed him inside, took his coat and hat and plunked him down at one of the tables.

"What'll it be? You hungry? Just thirsty?"

It was too early for dinner, but his stomach reacted to the smells from the kitchen. She grinned at him, patted his shoulder, and left him alone.

He rubbed his hands briskly to get them warm.

Although he liked this place pretty much, and didn't mind working for Maggie now and then, sweeping or hammering, stuff like that, it was better in the summer, when families came by and filled the dining room with their noise.

The silence made him nervous.

There wasn't enough light, there wasn't enough noise.

He cleared his throat hard, just for the sound.

He wondered what was keeping her? She could've skinned a buffalo already, and by now he was starving.

A finger scratched through his beard, then passed over his naked upper lip. Maybe it was time he grew a mustache too. He was looking too much like those Amish people; people would see him and get the wrong idea.

Especially Grayleen.

Then he heard Maggie whisper, "Dewey, my friend, I have something to show you."

FOURTEEN

Proctor sat motionless on the passenger side and stared out the window at the river below, ignoring the snap and blur of the bridge's passing girders. A rowboat drifted on the current, two men in dark gleaming slickers trolling. A family of ducks flew south, low over the surface.

Taz drove.

Neither had said a word since leaving the hospital, a small building equipped for only the basics; severe cases went elsewhere.

Nevertheless, they had to wait there for nearly an hour.

Are you sure you want to see this? Doctor Murloch had asked, a middle-aged, old-fashioned GP who doubled as the town coroner. They stood in a small room in the basement, the reek of formaldehyde and disinfectant, the murmur of an unseen air-conditioning unit. The overhead lighting was clear and harsh; and cold. Proctor had nodded, and the doctor, with a sympathetic glance, knew he was lying. Delany was on a gurney, covered by a fresh sheet; a ghost, he thought, at rest. With the thumb and forefinger of each hand the doctor peeled the sheet back off Delany's face.

That's him, was all Proctor said.

Sorry, both the doctor and Nathan said, not quite automatically.

More, Proctor ordered with an uncertain gesture.

The doctor balked.

No call, really, Nathan whispered.

More, he insisted.

The doctor shrugged, it was no skin off his back, and whipped the sheet away, held it in one hand.

Christ, Taz had said and turned away, a hand over his mouth.

Dried blood mottled the hairy chest; deep, erratic lacerations ranged from the hollow of his throat to his abdomen; welts, dozens of welts; a bulge in the crook of his left elbow where the shattered bone hadn't quite broken through; the left side of his face was severely scraped, nose smashed, left eye filled with blood.

Sometimes, the doctor explained dispassionately as he replaced the sheet, they get tossed to one side, or up and over; sometimes, like this one here, they get snagged underneath and are dragged for God knows how long. You'll make the arrangements? We don't have a whole lot of room here, I'm sorry.

Taz coughed.

Proctor rubbed a heavy hand over his face. We'll be staying at the Cumberland Motel, he said. You'll send me the death certificate?

The man checked with Nathan before nodding, cautiously. I'll send it over in the morning.

I appreciate it, he said, and reached out. Touched Delany's cold pale bare shoulder.

screaming

Taz coughed again, and said, come on, boss, let's go.

don't let them

Proctor shook himself, more inside than out, and looked up at the sheriff.

Nathan held his hat in both hands, solemn, respectful. Tensed as if expecting an outburst or grief or anger or accusation.

Proctor turned away without a word and let Taz lead him into the hall, up the stairs, through the lobby, into the fresh air and the glitter of mist on the grass.

Once over the bridge, Taz turned right sharply, tires squealing. He didn't apologize as he sped up, and Proctor didn't expect him to. Instead, he looked straight ahead and cautioned himself about jumping to conclusions. Right now he was numb, barely feeling the clammy chill that had seeped into the car. There were things that needed doing first; everything else had to be locked away for a while.

Locked away, but not forgotten.

When Crockston was behind them, the Kat Kave coming up, he looked over and saw Taz clenching his jaw, the muscle bulging and jumping.

"Slow down, Taz," he said quietly.

Taz nodded, and did. Barely.

Proctor faced front. "We'll get a room, freshen up, and then we'll figure out what next."

A hundred yards passed under the tires before Taz

said, "Why do they always say freshen up when they mean go to the john?"

Proctor's laugh was short and relieved. "It's a common consent thing. Go to the john is considered impolite in mixed company. So you say freshen up, or use the facilities, or powder my nose."

"I get it." Taz swerved around a rock in the middle of the lane. "Like, hit-and-run."

Surprised, and pleased, Proctor stared at him. Then: "Exactly."

He was surprised again at the inside of the motel. The small lobby was clean and smelled of lemon polish. Beyond the arched entrance to the dining room he saw a large family at one of the long tables, giggling, chatting, having a great, if quiet, time. Taz wandered to the entrance of the gift shop, glanced around, and wandered back with a *nothing special* shrug.

A woman behind the registration counter smiled at them warmly as she slid a form toward Proctor. "Staying long?" A nice voice; just right.

A couple of days, I think," Proctor told her, filling in the blanks.

"Well, I'll tell you, then, we don't have regular rooms, just the cabins. And the beds . . ." She swiped a stray hair away from her brow. "They're the double kind? Not very big? Unless you gentlemen like each other a lot, I'd recommend two places."

He grinned at what was obviously a well-worn joke. "Sounds good to me. The phones hooked up?"

She nodded, took his credit-card imprint, and reached under the counter for the keys. "Two and

Three. Lunch until four, dinner from five on. The museum is open . . ." She laughed shortly. "When it's open. If you want to go in, or you want something from the shop there, it's all from our local experts, just give me a holler. My name's Maggie. Maggie Medford."

One of the diners called her, and she excused herself, saying "You need anything in the room, you know where I am," and left with a small, flirtatious wave.

Taz said nothing until they were outside, on a flatstone walk that led from the steps to the cabins. "How come you didn't ask about Delany?"

"Later," he answered.

The first cabin was a good hundred feet from the main building. From the lamp glowing in the gap between drawn drapes in the window, he figured it was already occupied. He told Taz to take Number Three, get settled, and come over when he was ready; then he unlocked his door and stepped inside.

Silent.

Musty.

He let his bag drop, his eyes closed, and he said, "Oh, god," just before the tear fell.

Just one.

It didn't take long to unpack and explore.

The front room was, he estimated, about twenty-by-fifteen. A rectangular pine table under the front window, with two chairs, the phone, and a standing lamp in the corner, one hanging on a brass chain over the table itself. Pine-paneled walls without decoration. The bed was, as the woman had warned, barely worthy of the name double, extending from the right-hand wall to the room's center. Opposite it was a narrow dresser and a short stocky table with a TV on top. In back, a wide alcove opened onto two much smaller rooms—bath on the right, kitchenette on the left. The kitchenette had a door that opened onto a covered stoop and a hard-earth, crushed-stone parking area.

After using the bathroom, and dousing his face with cold water, he sat at the table and took a number of deep breaths before he called Lana.

As soon as she heard, she began to cry.

RJ took over, and Proctor gave her instructions without allowing her to ask questions: call in two of their part-timers, send them to Connecticut to get all the files from Blaine's questhouse. Copies or originals, he didn't care as long as they got them all in however many trips it would take. And make sure Doc went with them. Get as much of the material as they could into the computer. Set up a billing system for Blaine only. Get in touch with Vivian Chambers and make sure she understood how things worked.

Call the funeral parlor and make arrangements for Delany's body to be flown home; the burial would wait until he and Taz returned.

He did not know how long he would be in Kentucky; he would get home when he got home.

Lana came back on the line just as he heard a knock on the door. "It's open, Taz," he called.

Taz sat on the edge of the bed and listened, saying nothing.

"Kill the bastard," Lana commanded with cold heat.

He smiled grimly at the wall. "Sure."

"Skin him first, then kill him."

"Whatever you say."

"Forget it. When you catch him, call, and I'll send Chico down to haul him back. I'll do it myself."

He didn't doubt it, but he stopped her anyway, explained briefly about Blaine, and laughed when she asked if this meant she could buy her husband a new suit. "Armani, if you want," he said, "Then you explain to him how it figures to be an expense."

"No problem, Proctor. I can do it in my sleep."

The last thing she said was, "Catch the bastard, Proctor, catch him."

He slumped, sighed, and rubbed his eyes with the heels of his hands. Through the window he could see the walkway, a low line of tended shrubs, and the highway, the river, the ridge on the other side. He could feel the mountain rising behind the cabins. All that open sky, and he still felt as if he were in a box.

Finally he turned to Taz, who said, "There's a small refrigerator in that kitchen thing. If we're going to be a while, do you mind if I get some supplies from town later?"

"Sure, why not."

Taz still wore his jeans, but had changed into a black flannel shirt. He fussed with one of the buttons as he looked side to side without looking at Proctor.

Proctor waited. Taz wasn't used to working with someone else, not directly, and certainly not his boss. He didn't yet know what the ground rules were, and Proctor decided to let him figure them out for himself. He himself wasn't convinced yet that taking him

along was a good idea, or even why, really, he had
done it.

Taz wasn't the only one used to working alone.

"Do you—" Taz cut himself off, scratched vigorously through his hair, made an almost comical number of faces as he worked up to the first step.

Finally: "Do you think he was lying? The sheriff,
I mean."

Proctor didn't hesitate: "What do you think?"

Taz let his hands dangle between his legs. "I think
that was no hit-and-run, boss. I think it couldn't have
been. Delany didn't have a cell phone, and I didn't
see one of those roadside phone booths anywhere.
And he was on the phone when he . . . when it
started, whatever it was." He shook his head, doubt
still there. "I don't know if he was lying, or the doctor was, and I'm no expert on what people look like
after . . . after. But I think it didn't happen the way
they said."

"I know. You're right."

"I am?"

"Yep."

"Gee." Taz leaned back, propped on his elbows.
"Wow." He frowned at the ceiling. "But that
means . . ." He studied the ceiling, wall to wall. "Too
many questions."

"Pick one."

"Murder?" came out so fast he blinked, remembering that the subject had already come up once before.

"Animal?" Proctor countered. "Those injuries—he
wasn't dragged. Bear, maybe?"

"Inside?" Taz shook his head. "Who would have
a pet bear or something like that inside?"

"Space vampire."

"What?" Taz sat up. "Are you . . . oh. Information. As in, not enough of."

Proctor nodded.

"So why didn't you ask Maggie Medford about Delany then?"

Proctor glanced out the window, looked back, and tilted his head—*think about it, Taz, you already know.*

Taz checked the ceiling again, biting on his lower lip. "I said before . . ." He hesitated. "The museum thing. I said there'd be no way he'd pass this place up. The . . . the only other place we saw was by that bar." He looked at Proctor. "Not his style. He was in Crockston, so . . . so he was here."

Proctor nodded; *probably.*

Taz sighed. "More information, right? Lay of the land kind of thing." And when Proctor smiled, for his answer and impatience, he added, "So what about that woman then? She wanted to tell us something, I think, but the sheriff ran her off. Maybe we ought to try to—"

"Go in the kitchen."

"Huh?"

"Go in the kitchen an look outside."

Confused, he did as he was told. A moment later he called, "Hey, that old car is next door." He walked out of the kitchen, fingers snapping at his side. For the first time, Proctor realized he bounced a little, almost a strut, as if walking, or dancing, on the balls of his feet. "You think maybe . . ." and he tilted his head toward the wall.

"Yes," he said. "I think maybe our Miss Power is spending the night."

Taz feigned intense concentration and debate, rubbing his chin thoughtfully, nodding to himself, peering into the distance, before coming to a conclusion. "Well, you know, maybe we ought to kind of interview her, you know? I mean, she did act as if she had something to tell us."

Proctor immediately stared out the window, not daring to speak. One word, and he would explode into laughter which, he knew, would soon spiral out of control. He concentrated on the greylight that filled the river valley, on a car that sped north soundlessly, on the way the bushes between the cabin and the highway trembled as a breeze sifted through them.

Suddenly he felt old.

very old.

And very tired.

"Boss?"

Even his voice sounded old: "Don't call me that. Proctor will do fine."

He needed to rest. He wasn't superhuman. Too much too soon with too little sleep. Rest. Recharge. A time of absolute silence. Not to think, just to drift. He needed to rest.

He closed his eyes briefly, and saw Delany on the slab.

He opened his eyes and saw the greylight.

A long, slow sigh.

Rest.

Rest; then find out why the sheriff had lied.

FIFTEEN

Cory Nathan was not in the best of moods. As he drove out of the Kat Kave parking lot, he couldn't help a feeling he'd had a lot lately—that he should just chuck it all, pack his bags, and get the hell out of Dodge before the roof fell in.

The girls hadn't helped any, either.

No sooner had he returned from the hospital and settled himself at his desk, when Grayleen Simms called, damn near hysterical, babbling about some pervert sneaking around the woods back of the Kave. Normally, when there was an alarm from the strip bar, the deputy who took the call would leap to his feet, yell, "To the Batcave!", and run out to his cruiser. Unless Nathan decided to go himself. Then just about everyone in the office gave the yell, and waited until he either blew his stack, or snarled.

Then they would yell it again.

Today the dispatcher had said, "Disturbance at the Kave, Sheriff," and nobody had said a word.

Nobody wanted to go out there.

Nobody wanted to leave town.

What he expected when he arrived was someone like Dewey Plowman, lurking in the trees, hoping to catch a glimpse of one of the dancers on her break. Why, he had never been able to figure out, since all he had to do was go inside and see them practically buck-naked for not much more than the price of a damn beer. Dancing, too; not just standing around, smoking.

What he got, however, after a lot of poking around with his flashlight, water dripping down the back of his neck, was a goddamn deer. Not even a decent buck. A doe barely old enough to be called the name.

Grayleen, and beetle-brained Helly Trapp, insisted it wasn't a deer they had seen, they weren't that stupid, but he had no patience for them. He'd bitten their heads off, chewed Charity out for running a damn freak show, and left before he said something he'd really regret.

He headed for town deliberately slowly. His hands shook, and he gripped the wheel more tightly.

He was supposed to be the man folks looked up to in times of crisis; he was supposed to be the one who kept his head; he was supposed to be the one who, when he wasn't doing a million other things like keeping the law from falling apart, was supposed to keep those folks safe.

Today he wasn't any of those things.

This was *her* fault.

She should have called him, damnit; she should have warned him. That damn spur-of-the-moment story he'd come up with this time didn't hold water. He knew it. Those two men knew it, he could tell. And it was only a matter of time before they called him on it.

The older one especially.

There was something about him Nathan didn't like.

He wasn't all that big—not more than six foot, not a whole lot of visible muscle; and he wasn't one of them big-town, I'm hot shit and you're a country bumpkin kind of guys.

It wasn't that.

It was that there was an *age* about him—in his eyes, in that voice—that had unnerved him from the start. Like he knew stuff he shouldn't; like he'd seen stuff he didn't want to, and couldn't forget.

Like nothing the sheriff could tell him would be a real surprise. If, that is, he ever got around to telling him the truth.

"Crap," he muttered, and pressed the accelerator a bit, wishing he could take a few minutes, drop in at the General Lee and have himself a beer. Two. Three.

Whatever it took.

Out on the river he saw two men in a rowboat, huddled in slickers, and he had half a mind to pull over, get out the bullhorn and scream at them for being idiots. He knew they weren't local, had already seen them a couple of times today. Drifting south, trolling, using the motor to bring them back to the bridge where they started all over. On an ordinary day he would've gotten them to the bank and suggested they'd do better up around the bend, or 'way down near the interstate bridge. Undersize river bass, some lost trout, maybe once in a while a miserable pike was about all they'd get for their trouble around here. If they got anything at all.

But he didn't stop.

Not until he was caught by the first traffic light,

and sat there, stewing, glancing over at the corner and scowling at old Vickers sitting on the bus stop shelter bench. As if there really was a bus coming. Which there hadn't been for a couple of years. The old man was losing his grip. Time his family did something about it.

But when the light changed, he drove on.

It didn't make any difference how he felt, what he wanted; he had to get back to the office, make a stupid report, and suffer the ribbing of those who might still be at their desks.

Then he was going to call *her* and give her hell.

"Yeah," he muttered. "Sure you will."

Taz saw the police car pull out of the parking lot, and thought he recognized the sheriff at the wheel. He slowed down, giving the sheriff room, and glanced over at the bar. It was a temptation, but maybe later, when he had some free time.

He snorted a laugh.

No, probably not.

Proctor would find out for sure and fire his butt. Taz wouldn't have to say a word, wouldn't even have to have anything on his breath. The man would *know*.

Like he probably knew where Taz was now, even though he was in bed, supposedly sleeping.

How, he wondered, could the man sleep at a time like this? He'd said something about being fresh, but all Taz had ever gotten out of a nap was a splitting headache.

When the business district began, he realized he could be driving forever before he found what he wanted. Hardware store, barbershop, pizza place, real estate office, gas station on the corner, bank on the other corner. Dress shop, shoe store . . . he shook his head in disgust and pulled over when he saw an old man sitting in a bus-stop shelter. He rolled the passenger window down and leaned over the car's center armrest.

"Hi," he said.

The old man just looked at him. He wore a topcoat that looked too warm, a hat that didn't keep grey strands from escaping all around the brim, and pale leather gloves. His glasses distorted the size and color of his eyes.

"Sorry to bother you, but I'm looking for a supermarket or a 7-Eleven, something like that. Can you help me out?"

The old man blinked, but didn't speak. His hands were clasped tightly in his lap, and his feet were tucked under the bench, as if he wanted to run but couldn't find the nerve, or the strength.

He kept staring at the bridge.

Taz checked through the rear window to be sure no bus was about to rear-end him, then broadened the smile. "A tourist, you know?" He shrugged his helplessness.

Finally, slowly, the old man pointed over his shoulder.

"Thanks." Taz gave him a quick wave, and pulled around the corner; he looked back, but the old man didn't turn. He just sat there, huddled, not flinching at all when the downpour began; staring at the bridge.

Taz cursed and switched on the wipers. Just what

he needed. It was so hard, the drops sounded like pellets on the roof, and for a second he felt sure the windshield would crack. He was about ready to pull over and wait it out, when he saw the supermarket come up out of the rain on the right. He didn't bother to hunt for a parking lot. He parked in front and braced himself, then shoved the door open and ran for the entrance.

It didn't help.

He was drenched when he got inside, shivering a little from the cold water and the air-conditioning. The market was small, only a handful of people there, but no one looked at him as he hustled up and down the aisles, filling his arms with soda and snacks. A smile for the clerk was wasted. A "thanks" was wasted, too, as he bagged the groceries himself and ran out again.

"Brother," he said, once back behind the wheel.

He frowned then, and looked over.

They were there.

The clerk and five others, standing at the store window. Blurred by the rain.

Watching him.

He didn't know what to do, so he waved, felt like a jerk, and pulled away from the curb without looking. A horn startled him, making him swerve back into the curb, his shoulders hunching at the thump, his palms slipping around the wheel as he tried to regain control. Another car sped around him, honking angrily, filling the windshield with spray, blinding him so thoroughly he took his foot off the accelerator and let the car drift back to the curb a third time.

He sat there, shaking, cursing, wishing he were

back in Jersey where Doc would call him "Paul," and Proctor stayed behind that thick oak door.

They were still staring back there, he just knew it.

The rain pummeled the car.

The radio gave him nothing but static.

He turned on the headlights so other drivers would know he was there, then sang quietly and off-key to himself until the downpour eased and he could see the street reasonably well. The streetlamps were on. Neon sparkled in small shop windows. When he pulled away from the curb after checking the nonexistent traffic three times, he saw a school up ahead on the left, with a crescent driveway he decided to use to turn around in.

Then he saw the square brick building across the street, and grinned. It was too late now, the place looked closed, but he would make time tomorrow to drop in for a while. If the sheriff was lying now, maybe he had lied before, and Taz was pretty sure he'd either find out why, or how many times.

"Okay," he said loudly. "Way to go, way to go."

An involuntary glance over as he passed the supermarket again: the customers were gone, but the clerk was still there.

Staring at the rain.

Staring at him.

A gust of wind shuddered the car.

And the old man was still at the bus stop, little more than a shadow.

The sheriff sat in his office, door closed, and stared at the telephone, wondering if this was how it felt, burying yourself alive.

Get out of Dodge?

In your dreams, you old fool; should've thought of that years ago. Should have thought of that the very first day.

The second she had stepped out of that little airplane, spring wind blowing her hair, one hand shading her eyes, Cory Nathan knew he was going to fall in love with Jack Medford's wife-to-be.

And he had.

Hard as a man could without losing the will to live, because she wasn't his, and wasn't ever going to be.

Good friends, the three of them, was pretty good enough back then, though, and when Jack had died up there on Spooner Mountain, it was Cory she had called, screaming hysterically; it was Cory who trudged up that damn mountain, bile and ice in his gut, finding his buddy at the bottom of a fifty-foot drop, neck broken, scratched all to hell, places here and there where some critters had already gotten to him; it was Cory who had wrapped him in a blanket, then carried him back down the slope, weeping, with Maggie stumbling alongside; Cory who couldn't stand her red, puffy face, and all those tears, the leaves in her hair, hands violently trembling, as she begged him to let her bury him herself.

A special place, she'd said; *their* place.

He had hated himself, but he'd agreed because he still loved her, because he couldn't stand the awful pain in those eyes.

A hundred times a fool, but that was his cross to bear.

And he'd never asked where that special place was.

He sighed loudly, and dialed, and closed his eyes when she came on the line, remembering how it was. Before she changed.

"Maggie, I'm asking you . . . please . . . do not do this to me again."

"Asking, Corliss? Sounds to me like you're telling."

"Well, I'm sorry, but maybe it's because I'm a little angry here. Those men didn't believe a single word I said."

"So?"

"So? Maggie, have you lost your . . . Maggie, look, these men are different. I don't know how, and I don't know why, but they're bound to be trouble."

"Cory honey, there isn't a trouble on this earth you can't handle, you know that."

"Maggie, you're not listening to me."

"Oh, honey, you know that's not true."

"Will you stop it, please? Listen! One of those men is that guy's boss, you hear me? He says he came down because one of the state cops called him, told him about the accident. He's the only family that guy has."

"Cory. Honey. I don't see the problem. Don't you think you might be overreacting, just a little?"

"Maggie. Honey. I didn't notify the state to keep an eye out for damaged vehicles until nine, maybe ten. You listening now? Nine, maybe ten. Those men rolled in here around noon. From New Jersey. You want to figure it out, or should I do it for you?"

"No, Cory. I get it."

"I hope so, I truly hope so. Because if you don't, and I lose this election because these folks decide I can't handle the situation anymore, I ain't gonna be able to protect you anymore, and that's no lie."

She was laughing when he hung up, and he sat for a long while, hands over his eyes.

Grayleen tugged her sweater more snugly around her shoulders, shivering, feeling the goose bumps rise on her legs. She stood at the rear fire exit, one knee holding it open so she could blow the cigarette smoke out, thinking for the hundredth time it was a damn dumb rule that the men out front could smoke themselves to death, but it was a fire hazard or something for the girls to smoke in their laughable excuse for a dressing room.

Rain spilled in sheets off the roof.

The woods simmered and shifted.

The music out front was muffled; she felt more than heard the old-fashioned, heavy, bump-and-grind bass. Charity's idea. Anyone can move around to rock music, she'd said; it takes a real pro to work to the real thing.

Grayleen hated it, but the customers loved it.

And tonight she intended to work extra hard, make them love her too. Because the one thing she damn well wasn't going to do was leave the Kave alone.

The word was out.

The night wasn't safe.

SIXTEEN

Proctor sat at the table.

The nap, or what there had been of it, was exactly what he had needed. No dreams. No images of Delany. No . . . man in the snow. He had taken a quick shower after waiting forever for the hot water to kick in, pretended that his brush knew what to do with his hair, and slipped into a matching dark shirt and jeans. Noting with faint dismay that he could probably get away with not wearing a belt.

Then he turned on the light that hung over the pine table, thought about it for a moment, and turned all the lights on, including the bathroom and kitchenette. He pulled the drapes open. He unlocked the door. He made sure that sitting at the wall end of the table didn't make him invisible to anyone walking by, or anyone who came to the door.

The rain made the lights seem all that much more warm. A none too subtle invitation. Just in case his neighbor wanted to talk.

Then he braced himself and called Lana.

It wasn't as bad as he'd feared; She was her old self, more or less.

She had already contacted Vivian Chambers and

arrangements had been made to ship the files to the office. "Proctor, do you really think you can find her? After all this time?"

"I'll do my best, Lana. He knows it's a long shot."

"No," she said sadly, "I don't think he really does."

He had no answer.

"I talked with Franklin Blaine, too. He's going to oversee the shipping. Stuffy, you know? But kind of nice, in a way. He doesn't like this."

"I know."

"But he wants his father at peace. He'll help, him and his sister."

Proctor nodded, not willing to admit he felt relieved at the news. "Okay, good. Anything else?"

There was nothing in the mail she couldn't handle on her own; Doc was annoyed Taz had gone instead of him, "but he'll get over it"; Shake Waldman hadn't called back, no great loss as far as she was concerned; the phone machine tapes had been duplicated, the originals gone to the safety-deposit box in the bank, copies in the office safe; it was raining like crazy, the squirrels had been playing on the porch all day anyway, and if Proctor didn't come home soon, she was going to have Chico wring their little ratty necks.

Then: "Are you all right?"

"No. And yes."

"How long?"

"As long as it takes."

A long pause before she said, "I listened to the tape again."

He waited, reaching to the pane to touch the glass; it was cold.

"Be careful," was all she said before she said good-bye.

He cradled the receiver and watched the soft rain. By the clock it wasn't yet night, but it was night out there now, and there was no traffic on the highway. A slow wind scattered droplets on the window; he could see their ghosts sliding across the backs of his hands.

It was an image he didn't appreciate, and he pulled his hands away, but the ghosts remained, on the table this time.

Then he frowned and leaned forward, trying to see as far to the left as he could. His head tilted. The frown deepened.

Someone was out there.

Someone was watching.

It was neither nerves nor reaction; the cabin was being watched.

When the kitchen door slammed open, he snapped his head around, holding his breath until Taz strode in, a shopping bag in each arm.

"Do you think that maybe now," the kid said as he dropped the groceries on the bed, "we could afford a damn umbrella?"

Proctor watched as items were displayed for his approval, nodding at the six-pack, shrugging at the twelve-pack of soda, making a face at the diet soda.

"Good," Taz said. "This stuff is poison. What'll I do with it?" Without waiting for an answer, he carted everything into the kitchenette and put it away, complaining about the size of the refrigerator, muttering about the cupboard, telling him he'd already left some beer and stuff in his own cabin, he hoped Proctor didn't mind.

Constant movement, constant talk, and despite all the lights, the rain ghosts still snaked across the table.

He glanced at the window.

The watched feeling was gone.

Nerves, after all.

When Taz was done, he dropped a couple of newspapers on the bed, stood in the middle of the room and looked around. Anxious. Ready. No more naps, no more talks. "So . . . now what?"

Proctor pushed away from the table. "Now we have dinner. Go dry your hair, make yourself pretty."

"Then what?"

"We walk."

"Then why bother with my hair? We still don't have umbrellas."

Proctor picked up the first section of one of the papers and held it over his head. "Instant umbrella. It's not raining that hard."

The kid muttered something under his breath and disappeared into the bathroom, complained loudly about the thin towels, yelled something about something he wanted to do the next day, and returned to find Proctor already at the door. Still muttering, he followed him outside, was about to break into a trot, when Proctor grabbed his arm.

"Walk," he ordered, ignoring Taz's running commentary on the weather and the lower temperature, until they stopped in front of the first cabin. "Wait," he said, and climbed onto the stoop.

Knocked twice, and waited.

When the door opened, he said, "Miss Power, my friend and I would be pleased if you'd join us for dinner."

They sat at the far end of the first long table, Proctor facing Taz and the woman, whose backs were to a multipaned window. The dining room was dimly lit, the furniture toward the back wall more suggestion than seen. The brightest light was in the lobby; the gift shop was dark.

Maggie greeted Proctor with a friendly smile as she wiped her hands on a short wrinkled apron, asked if the cabins were all right, and told him there was no menu. Roast beef or meat loaf, vegetables and potatoes, all on platters and bowls; each diner served himself. "What you see is what you'll get. Apple and peach pie for dessert."

He nodded. She smiled at Taz, and left.

After a moment he said, "Well, I guess you two don't get along."

Flower grimaced. "She thinks I'm a slut." She wore a man's flannel shirt buttoned to the neck, and jeans he figured were a good size too large. "Because I dance," she added. Then, abruptly, she smiled. "She probably thinks you two and me are gonna party later."

Proctor glanced at an openmouthed Taz, pointed a finger, and said, "Don't."

Taz immediately shook his head in such a blatant declaration of innocence that Proctor laughed, picked up his fork, and tapped it against his forearm. "Now tell me with a straight face that your real name is Flower."

Flower folded her arms on the table. "I thought we were gonna talk."

"We are. But I'd rather eat first, all right? It's been a long, lousy day . . . and I'm not going anywhere, anytime real soon." He passed a forefinger lightly across his brow, down his cheek. "I think better when I'm relaxed. And I relax when I eat."

He watched her carefully, knowing she was in the midst of a debate, probably wondering if maybe she had made a mistake.

"Lulu," she said at last.

Taz gaped. "What?"

"Lulu. My real name is Lulu." She giggled. "Hell of a thing to be stuck with, huh?"

"Flower is good," Taz said quickly.

"Flower Power is better," Proctor added. He held up the peace sign. "War kills children and other living creatures."

Flower blinked once, very slowly, almost a wink. "You're not old enough, Mr. Proctor."

"Proctor," Taz corrected sourly. "You call him mister and he gets all bent out of shape."

"If I'm Lulu," she said, "fair's fair, who are you?"

"Ethan."

"I like it."

He held the fork still. "I like Proctor better."

"See?" said Taz. "What'd I tell you?"

"You're not old enough either," Proctor said.

She covered a smile with her fingers and shook her head. "You lie pretty good, you know that?"

"Comes in handy sometimes, for what I do for a living."

"And what," she asked, "is that?"

"Hey," Taz complained, "remember me?"

The food came, and Proctor leaned back to allow Maggie to set the bowls and platter down. She talked the whole time, explaining how to get seconds, how to get dessert, did they want their meals put on their bill; she brushed Proctor's shoulder with one hand, brushed fingers over Taz's wrist as she reached over to take his fork—"I'll get you a clean one, hon, this one's a reject"—and stood back with arms folded contentedly over her chest to survey the table.

"Everyone happy?"

Taz, reaching for the meat loaf, looked up awkwardly. "Any chance the museum is open?"

"Not now, hon. Have to wait until dinner's over."

"Okay. Thanks."

A single nod that she was pleased, a bright smile, and she turned to leave just as Proctor said, mildly, "Delany." She paused and looked quizzically over her shoulder.

"Friend of mine," he said, scooping mashed potatoes onto his plate. "He may have dropped in—for the museum, you know?—sometime this week."

She frowned in concentration, then shrugged a *sorry I don't know him* apology, jokingly reminded Taz to eat his vegetables, and walked away.

"I'm a ghost," Flower said resentfully. She stared at her empty plate. "A ghost and a whore in this godforsaken town."

Taz, after a glance at Proctor that brought no response, pulled at the side of his neck. "Then why are you staying here, if you hate her so much?"

"Cory," she said, a one-handed shrug. "Sheriff Nathan. Called her and told her to put me up. Something about the case, I guess, I don't know." She scanned the room; another shrug. "Better'n that roach motel by the Kave, though, I suppose." A mischievous smile, fleeting. "Pisses her off, the only good thing about it."

Proctor reached over and touched her hand. "Later," he said gently. "Eat now. Put on a couple of useful pounds."

She looked at him without raising her head, then looked at Taz. "He always this good?"

Straight-faced, he answered, "Hell, he's just warming up."

Proctor mock-glared, and they ate. A few questions about them, a few about her, a few about the town. Nothing serious, nothing distressing.

Nothing he didn't know or hadn't figured out already.

Friday night in Crockston, with rain pattering against the window.

When the meal was over, the dishes cleared away, Proctor leaned back and sighed with content, one hand resting on his stomach. This was one of the benefits of traveling the way he did—unexpected pleasures in out-of-the-way places. Fancy had little to do with what was put upon your plate.

"Well," he said, and Flower smiled back.

Behind him he could hear someone pushing a broom across the floor. He checked lazily over his shoulder and saw a small man in bib overalls making his way between the table rows, keeping his mind on his task as if it were the most important work in the world. A beard but no mustache, wiry unruly hair that curled around his ears and nape.

And outside, he realized, the rain had finally stopped.

"Well," he said again.

A clatter behind him made him look quickly. The man in overalls had dropped his broom, staring at Flower and blushing. "I . . ." He grabbed the broom and held it to his chest. "Sorry, folks. I . . . sorry," and hustled away into the kitchen.

When Proctor turned around, Flower's face had changed.

"You know him?"

She nodded brusquely. "Name's Dewey. I see him a lot." A hand gestured vaguely. "You know."

"So," Taz said before Proctor could stop him, "are you, uh, going to work tonight?"

She looked at him to see if he was leering, or suggesting, or ready to judge.

He blushed too, and stammered nonsense because he didn't know if he should apologize or not.

She bumped his shoulder with hers. "Don't worry about it, it's all right. And no, I'm not. I'm done for the season." She explained how it worked: the town leaders want a cleanup, the sheriff warns the least offenders before his men hit the roundup road, and she packs up and heads to Memphis for the winter. "Would've been there by now, too." She smiled wanly. "Just my luck."

"Yeah," Taz said, "but then you wouldn't have met us."

She groaned. "Oh, Lord, not him too."

Proctor smiled as he pushed away from the table. "We ate, I'm relaxed, let's take a walk. Taz, lend the lady your coat. It's little chilly outside."

To his credit, Taz didn't say a word. Flower protested only until he held it out and shook it once; then she shrugged into it with his help and walked between them to the porch.

The air smelled of fresh rain and damp leaves; the wind had settled into a slow whispering breeze. A van hissed south on the highway. Another raced in the opposite direction, its headlights turning all the leaves grey.

Proctor slipped his hands into his pockets, nodded toward the cabins, and as they went down the steps, he said, "Tell me about Delany."

SEVENTEEN

It didn't take very long.

With Proctor and Taz flanking her, she walked slowly toward the cabins and explained how and where she'd found the body, called the sheriff, and made her statement.

"No call for me to stay," she said, "but then he found out y'all were coming and asked me to stick around, like I said."

They were beyond the reach of the motel lights, not yet in the glow of her cabin-door light. Dripping water the only sound, yet her head jerked birdlike every few seconds as if she heard something else. She did it so often Proctor couldn't help looking himself.

By the time they reached the cabin, he was ready to grab her just to keep her still.

"What is it?" he asked quietly when she hesitated.

Her hands were jammed deep into the jacket's pockets; she wouldn't look up. He could feel her struggling again, unsure whether she should tell him or not.

He glanced at Taz, who shrugged and took a silent sliding step away, heading back toward his own cabin.

Proctor waited.

Water dripped.

Flower shook her head helplessly, still staring at the ground.

Proctor wanted to reassure her, to tell her she had nothing to fear from him. Twice he opened his mouth, and twice he closed it. The night's chill had slipped under his clothing, but he ignored it.

Finally, hands still in his pockets, he leaned forward, his brow nearly touching the top of her head. "Listen," he said, almost a whisper, "I know he wasn't hit by any car."

She jumped, kept her head down.

"I know things," he continued, "that ordinary, sane people wouldn't believe in broad daylight."

This time she didn't move.

"Whatever it is, if you're afraid of it, that's okay." He took a breath. "Is it possible we're talking here about something like a bear? Are there wildcats in these mountains? Mountain lions?" Another breath. "Somebody escaped, a killer maybe, and the sheriff is too embarrassed to admit it or call in anyone else, because he can't catch him on his own." Another breath. "Something else."

She did look up then, and they were so close he could feel her breath on his chin. He didn't smile; neither did she. He didn't move away; neither did she.

Then: "People die here, Proctor," in a voice as quiet as his. "They go hunting and don't come back, they come out of the mine and never get home. Sometimes they find the bodies, sometimes they don't." Her shoulders hunched against the breeze, but she didn't look away. "They say folks get lost, they say accidents happen all the time, they say these mountains ain't as friendly as they look, they say people who live back in the hollers don't like other folks nosing around." She glanced at Taz, looked toward the motel. "All that's true, most of the time. But not all. And I'll tell you this, those people in the hollers? For the next couple of nights, every one of them'll have a gun."

She waited.

He didn't answer. He watched her eyes move back and forth, searching his face for signs of a twitch, a laugh, a scoffing.

She said, "I have a gun."

He didn't blink.

"I don't know that it'll do me any good."

He nodded. Very slowly.

She shifted her feet, lowered her head, lifted it again; a lopsided smile, uncertain and trembling.

"You gonna kiss me?"

He did, light and quick.

She stepped away then, startled and abruptly shy, turned and went to her door. He waited until she unlocked it and stepped inside before he straightened, cleared his throat, and wondered what in hell he had just done.

She called his name.

When he looked, she was in the doorway, the overhead light out, a shadow in the lamp that shone behind her.

"No bear, Proctor," she said. "It wasn't no bear."

* * *

Lying in bed promised him no sleep, but he had already tried reading the papers Taz had bought, tried finding something on the mostly static television, tried convincing himself he should get dressed and get out again. Let the fresh air keep him awake while he did his best to think.

As soon as Flower had closed the door, the sound of the bolt turning over like a whipcrack in the silence, he walked over to Taz, who had said, "Well, if it wasn't a bear or something, what the hell was it?"

He had no answer then.

He had no answer now.

Tomorrow, on the other hand, someone had better give him an answer or . . .

Or what, Proctor?

You going to hold your breath until you turn blue? Call in the cavalry? Call the *New York Times* and spill this little town's dirty little secrets? Of which, in case you've forgotten, you don't know squat? Like it would matter anyway?

The wind came up and something rolled across the shingles.

The cabin sprang drafts that forced him to pull the blanket closer to his chin.

If it wasn't a bear, if Flower was right, then what are we talking about here, smart guy? Border-state Sasquatch? Killer alien from Mars hiding out in the mountains? A psychopathic murderer who uses homemade claws for his weapon of choice? Maybe something in the river, the Hideous Creature from the Kentucky Black Lagoon?

Why in God's name did you kiss her, Proctor?

She was joking, for crying out loud. You were so

close, you could smell her skin, smell her hair, you almost went cross-eyed.

Why the hell did you kiss her?

He closed his eyes, but he couldn't stop thinking.

He opened his eyes and yelped, sat up so fast he made himself dizzy.

Taz stood at the foot of the bed, a knife in one hand, a manic grin on his face.

Proctor rammed himself against the headboard, each breath short and shallow, looking wildly to the door, to the bathroom, back to the front door.

And Taz said proudly, "An umbrella, can you believe it? I found it in the trunk." He walked over to the window and yanked on the drape cord, and Proctor yelped again when morning exploded into the room. "I'm hungry, you want breakfast?"

Then: "Hey, boss, you okay?"

He asked it again thirty minutes later, after Proctor was out of a long, alternately hot and cold shower, adding, "No offense, but you look like shit. You get drunk last night, or what?"

Proctor only growled.

When he asked it a third time they were in the diner, in the same booth, but now the room was half-filled with customers and the place didn't seem so hollow.

The same waitress took their order, this time not so distant, and after his second cup of coffee, Proctor said, "Taz, for crying out loud, I'm okay, okay? And no," he added as Taz raised his hands in surrender,

"I did not get drunk. I just didn't sleep very well, that's all."

When he had looked out the back door, the old Mercedes was gone, and Taz hadn't mentioned her once, not even in innuendo.

Most of the clouds were gone, and those that were left were being shredded by a wind that lifted whitecaps on the river and made flags sound like gunshots. An autumn sky and autumn foliage that made the town look downright bucolic. A flurry of leaves tumbled up the street. An old woman walked her terrier past the diner, a much younger man at her side, bending over as if to listen. On his left hip his stained coat was hitched behind the large leather-wrapped shaft of what had to be a bowie knife. He wasn't bragging; it was out there for quick use.

"He might as well have a holster and a six-gun," Taz said. "Man, can you believe this place?"

Proctor watched until the window no longer framed them, looked down at his eggs-and-toast, then over at Taz's plate, which he figured would feed something the size of a small army. He had worn his lined denim jacket today, and changed into his jeans, which were no better than the chinos—he could have gone without the belt—and watching Taz eat made him waver between envy and disgust.

"Disgusting," he said at last, nodding toward the plate.

"Yeah." Taz grinned. "Ain't that great?" He wiped his mouth with a napkin, pushed the plate to one side, and picked up his coffee. "I want to go to the library today."

Proctor frowned.

"Well, if what the lady said was right, I'd probably find something in the back papers, you know? Maybe there's a pattern, maybe they already caught someone who did that other stuff."

"Okay, good idea." He nodded. "I'll go with you."

Taz shook his head. "No offense, boss—"

"Proctor."

"—but the mood you're in today, if you can't find anything, you'll slit the librarian's throat. Or mine." He lifted his hands at Proctor's astonishment—*well, it's true, isn't it?*—and suggested that Proctor walk up to the cop shop and talk to the sheriff while he was gone. They could meet later, and compare notes.

"And what if I'm done before you?"

Taz grinned smugly. "Patience, right? You wait here with patience."

"Or," Proctor said, "I could walk to the library and join you."

"That's a plan, too."

Proctor shook his head, folded his hands, and rested them on the table. A check of the other diners, a glance at the entrance, and he said, "Taz, look, the reason I brought you with me—"

"I was wondering."

"—is that I need you around when I talk to people. You listen. You see things. I'm not going to have that advantage if I see Sheriff Nathan on my own. Or anyone else, for that matter."

Flustered, Taz fussed with his cup, his water glass, reached over and plucked a packet of sweetener from its bowl. An argument was there, but he didn't know how to present it.

Proctor felt sorry for him. "I never needed you before, right?"

Taz wavered, then nodded.

"Delany didn't die before, either." He touched his chest with a finger. "I can't trust myself yet, Taz. It's still sinking in, and I'm still . . ." He shrugged. "You know."

"The library stuff is important," Taz insisted quietly. "Even if there isn't anything there, that's important."

"Doc, right?"

"No. You."

Proctor leaned back and studied the younger man. Flattery aside, he knew it was Doc and Lana who gave him lessons when he wasn't around. Like the space vampire picture. It had been Lana and Chico who had brought Taz to him, and Doc who had finally told him that the kid was all right, could be trusted, could be good.

"Then we're stuck," he said evenly. "Two guys, one car. We'll do the library first, then see the sheriff. And that doctor."

"Okay," Taz said reluctantly. "But if you kill the librarian, I ain't hiding the body."

Proctor laughed silently, caught the waitress's eye and signaled for the check. Then he took out his credit card and slid it over. "I," he said, sliding out of the booth, "am going to use the facilities."

In the men's room he gripped the worn sides of the basin and stared into a mirror whose glass was edged with dust. He looked better, he felt better, and why hadn't he thought of the library angle?

Because he was angry.

Still angry.

The grieving would come later.

He washed his hands, splashed a palmful of water on his face, took several deep breaths, and returned to the booth.

Where Flower looked up from his seat, and said, "I understand you could use a ride."

EIGHTEEN

"This is Kentucky!" Proctor complained loudly. "It's supposed to be the South. It's not supposed to be the middle of a goddamn Vermont winter in the middle of goddamn October."

His collar was up, a baseball cap was jammed down as far as it would go, his hands were bunched in his pockets, and his legs felt as if they had been frozen solid from the knees down. The sun was high, but it didn't do much good, not down here in the valley where the wind was an express train using the river for its tracks.

"Oh, stop your bitching," Flower called back from the warmth of the Mercedes idling on the shoulder on the other side.

He gave her a sour look, stamped his feet to bring them back to life, and continued walking, his back to the wind. He had started at the tunnel, had examined the roadside by painfully cold inches, every so often crouching to get a closer look. There were no illusions. Any remnants of the supposed accident would have been washed away by the rain. Still, there might be something—a bit of glass, a piece of cloth . . . and he had had to see the site. Just to be there. Just in case.

Leaves twisted around his ankles.

A candy wrapper clung to the back of his knee until he slapped it away.

He didn't stop until Flower signaled he had reached the spot where she had stopped as well. Then he turned into the wind and faced the bulge of Spooner Mountain that held the tunnel, instant tears, lips tight.

No phone booth, no pole to hold a roadside emergency phone, no nearby houses on either side of the tunnel, no shacks . . . no skid marks.

Delany had been dumped here.

On the other side of the road the slope rose sharply, thick with a forest that vibrated in the wind. He walked over without bothering to check for traffic and found no sign of footpaths or trails.

When the wind stopped abruptly, there were a few seconds of falling leaves that sounded like distant rain.

"I've seen enough," he said gruffly as he got in the car. Sunlight flared off the hood and the river, making him squint, threatening instant headache. He unzipped the coat and pulled a pair of sunglasses from his shirt pocket, slipped them on, and pointed with his chin. "Next stop."

"Sheriff?"

"Doctor."

She neither argued nor agreed; she just pulled away, taking it slow, letting him look. She hadn't explained where she had gone that morning, and with a look dared him to ask why she'd volunteered. He hadn't. He'd only thanked her.

"He'll warn the sheriff, you know," she said as they entered the tunnel. "Won't that make it worse?"

He yanked his cap off and flipped it into the backseat. "The sheriff will be tough anyway. If we talk to him first, he'll get mad probably, maybe figure it out and call whatshisname, Murloch, maybe scare him away." He grinned without mirth. "This way I get to scare him first."

She laughed. "Can you be scary?"

He didn't look at her. "Yes."

Nothing had gone right for Dewey since the second he woke up. The furnace didn't work, so he had no hot water, so he had to take a cold shower and shave in cold water, and when he got to the motel, Maggie had yelled at him without raising her voice, telling him what a jerk he was, why couldn't he do anything simple without screwing it up, even though it had been her damn dumb idea in the first place.

Well, damnit, he thought as he trudged angrily through the woods, it wasn't his fault he couldn't hear what they were saying. He was supposed to sweep and listen at the same time, but it was a new broom with a slippery handle, and when *she* had looked straight at him when he dropped it, he couldn't stand it.

And when he told Maggie what he had heard, nothing but weather talk and crap, she damn near kicked him out into the rain.

Then today she wants him to go through their rooms, see what he can find, and that was it, he drew the line. No way he was going to be in there if that guy came back, wanted to know what he was doing.

No way he was going to look into those eyes.

So he quit, and she yelled some more, and that was really damn scary because she hardly ever lost her temper, and she hardly ever yelled.

He was gone.

Took the cash she gave him like she was handing shit to a beggar, and he was gone.

Just as well.

He reached a small clearing just east of the motel and stood at its edge. More bare earth than grass, but nothing looked disturbed. The trap hadn't been sprung.

He moved on, up the slope, glad at least that the wind had stopped blowing. He hated the wind. Things came at you when you were in the trees and the wind was blowing and there was so much noise you could barely hear yourself walking; things came at you, and more than once he'd been whomped by a flying or falling dead branch.

They came at you, and you never even heard them coming.

An hour later he reached level ground. The trees were sparse here, no brush to speak of. He moved carefully, seeing signs of deer, maybe one of them damn Tennessee boars, not much else. The trap was still ready.

He rubbed his gloved hands together, reached into his old hunter's coat, and pulled out a flask. A quick sip, a shudder, and he put it back.

Screw Maggie Medford.

He had a feeling that today he was going to get rich.

*   *   *

Taz felt sick to his stomach, like being caught on
a ship in a hurricane.

He had opened his big mouth, had this big crime-
solving idea, and how was he to know that a library
in a hole like this would have a new microfilm machine that zipped by pages so fast he felt as if he
were falling. How was he also to know that the
county and the state had decided a while back that
small-town newspapers were worth saving on this
stuff. It apparently didn't matter that most of the
news had to do with school-board votes and tobacco
crops and mine surveys, bridge repair and river
dredging and ways to lure tourists into this particu-
lar section of the Cumberland Mountains; not to
mention honor rolls and bears wandering through
town looking for mates and someone claiming he'd
caught a northern pike in the river.

It was, the librarian had told him, a preservation
of history. Small towns, she had said, are where big
towns go when they get tired of big towns.

Southern wisdom, he thought grumpily; man, I
wish I had a decent pizza.

The trick, the woman had told him, reaching
around his shoulder, is to ease the knob, not spin it.
Spin it, you're going to heave on my floor and I'll
be darned if I'm going to clean it up.

She smelled of fresh soap and shampoo, was an
outrageous flirt even though he figured her to be at
least twice his age, and was constantly telling him
how grateful she was that he wasn't a schoolkid from
across the street, bent on the complete destruction of
her domain.

"Disgrace," she had muttered as she pretended not

to be trying to read his notes. "All they want is their video TV and those hand-game gizmos. At least you seem to have been taught some library appreciation."

He admitted that he had, stretched a little to get the kinks out of his back, and casually dropped his hand over the pad. If she noticed, she didn't react.

Two hours so far, and he had a feeling that Proctor would like what he'd found. No, he thought then; Proctor would be interested. Like had nothing to do with any of this.

What he didn't think he'd be able to explain is how empty the place felt. How deserted. There were no kids in the stacks, no old people reading the papers, no browsers at all, and there hadn't been since he'd arrived.

And the librarian wouldn't leave him be, as if she were afraid to be left alone.

Dewey glanced at the sun just as his stomach protested. He was hungry, practically starving, but he had one trap more to check before he could get himself some lunch. He hustled down a narrow trail that would eventually bring him close to the Kave. It was too early for the girls, though, which disappointed him some. He had a feeling they knew when he was watching, posing for him even while they were mocking him.

He didn't mind.

Whatever he could get without paying for it was okay with him.

The trap was still set.

That was okay, too.

Lucky was the name of this day today.

Rich, a hero, and maybe even famous.

Life was good.

But he crossed his fingers just the same.

At Proctor's request, Flower kept her speed well below the posted limit, pulling over whenever another car wanted by. In spite of the sun, and the shattered light on the water, he could see that the woods beyond either bank were too thick to let in much light; as if, back there, it was always late afternoon. When they passed the motel, it seemed set in pale shadow.

He faced forward, giving the bridge of his nose a weary two-finger massage.

Where did it happen? he asked a tattered leaf quivering in the wiper well; where did it get you?

And then Flower said without preamble, "You know, people make fun of the folks that live here, places like this, places back in the hills. Like they're not real people? Like because they believe some things and not others, they don't have all their minds? Think they're a bunch of superstitious hillbillies ain't got the brains God gave a snail.

"I started coming here about six, seven years ago. Stay a while, go away, come back, leave for the winter because they get kind of rowdy here when there isn't much to do. I never thought much of it before, but every once in a while the town hunkers in on itself, pulling into a shell if you know what I mean. I didn't make any connections one way or the other until a few years ago, four maybe, when this man, I think his name was Vickers, they found his wife in the river, caught under the bridge. Tore up all to hell.

Paper said she must have fallen in and got caught by blades, you know? Some guy's boat? I remember because it was a Saturday, my last day before heading home for the year.

"Nobody came to the Kave that night, Proctor.

"We girls who aren't from around here, like Grayleen Simms, a couple of others, we stayed in that fleabag motel next to the club. Charity, she's in charge, when it was pretty obvious we weren't gonna have any kind of show at all, she bundled us all back to our rooms and paid some boys to stand outside all night.

"All night, Proctor. Shotguns, rifles, knives, every damn thing you can think of.

"Scared the hell out of me, I can tell you that. I almost didn't come back."

They passed the Kave, no cars in the lot.

"So why did you?" he asked.

Her laugh was part bitter, part resigned. "Proctor, in case you hadn't noticed, I am not now, and haven't been for a while, a spring chicken. The kiss of death in my line of work. So Charity calls, I come on by. Girl has to make a living, you know."

"They catch the guy with the boat?"

She looked at him so long he had to gesture to get her to face the road again.

"No boat, Proctor. Never was a boat, if you listen to the people everyone else always makes fun of. She hadn't been gone but a few hours, so it wasn't fish nibbling at her either. I asked Cory about it, and he tells me not to worry my pretty little head about it. Rumors, he tells me, grow like weeds in this town. Cut back one place, they pop up in another. Funny

thing is, though, every time some idiot gets lost or
has an accident or just goes away without telling anyone, he's always around, making sure we're all right,
that we're not planning any camping trips or hiking
trips, stuff like that. Like I'm the type who wants to
sleep on the ground in a tent in the woods."

The car drifted onto the shoulder and stopped, her
hands on the wheel, eyes straight ahead.

"The thing is, Proctor, if you want to find out what
happened to your friend, you can't laugh at them.
You can't even think about laughing at them. They're
not gonna tell you shit anyway, but they sure won't
say anything if they think you're patting them on
the head."

His nod thanked her for the advice.

A trailer truck grumbled past, buffeting the car
with its backwash.

His voice, when he spoke, was steady and deep:
"What do they call it, Flower?"

"Call what?" As if she didn't know what he was
talking about.

"The whatever it is the people I'm not laughing at
call what makes people disappear, or gets them
killed."

She pursed her lips; her hands didn't leave the
wheel. "I don't think they call it anything." She
looked over at him. "You give something a name, it
kind of makes it more real."

Dr. Murloch, the receptionist told him politely but
sternly, was on his rounds, and he would either have
to take a seat and wait, or come back later. She had

no idea how long it would take, but the doctor didn't skimp when it came to taking care of his patients.

The implication was: bother him at your peril, and that starts with me.

She had tight white curls fresh from the beauty parlor, a light cardigan under her white smock, and a pair of glasses that hung against her ample chest on a glittering cord. He had met this woman before in a number of places—adamant and protective, fiercely so, and with a tight-lipped temper to match. He tried flattery, small talk, a sense of urgency, and hints of official disapproval. None of it worked.

He asked her to remind the doctor that he was waiting for copies of the death certificate he'd been promised for that morning. For his friend, who, he was sure she remembered, had been found on the road just the day before.

She didn't drop a single stitch. The automatic sympathy was there, but the permission wasn't.

Wait, or go. And she set her chin.

Then, relenting a little, she said, suddenly motherly and understanding, "If you're hungry, dear, try the Blue Sky Diner. They have some real nice food there. Or you could pass a little time at the museum. You know about our museum? Maggie Medford runs it. It's got some really interesting things. You go on over, dear, I'm sure the doctor'll be available by the time you get back."

Proctor stared at her.

If he didn't think it would scare her half to death, he would have leaned over her fortress desk and planted a big one on those wrinkled, too-red lips.

Instead, he thanked her, gave her his best smile, and nearly ran out the door.

"What?" Flower asked anxiously, waiting on the steps.

"I'm an idiot," he said as he grabbed her arm and hustled her to the car. "Hit me, I'm an idiot."

NINETEEN

They stepped into silence.

The curtains had been drawn over the dining-room windows, and the wagon-wheel lights had not been turned on. In the gift shop a small bulb over the door barely reached the first display case. And the carriage lamps on either side of the registration counter were just bright enough to make everything else darker.

Not a sound.

With one finger up to caution Flower not to speak, he eased over to the counter, leaned over and scanned the shelf below.

It was clean: no receipts, no box for forms, no folders, nothing. Just a telephone, and a cylinder wrapped in leather for ballpoints and pencils.

So much, he thought, for miracles.

When the paneled door opened in back, he leaned quickly on his forearms and smiled a broad good afternoon. Maggie didn't start, didn't blink; she smiled back after a quick glance at Flower, the kind, he thought, you give a bum on the street, one that turns him instantly invisible.

"Problem?" she asked, one eyebrow up. "You looking for some lunch?"

In the silence her voice was cotton soft.

"The guy I asked you about last night? My friend?"

Her expression sobered with concern. "I've been thinking about that, you know?" She pressed her thighs against the shelf, putting her so close he had to look up to see her face. "The thing is, Mr. Proctor, I just don't get that many guests this time of year. Hunters mostly, I had a couple in the middle of the week, but that's all. Sorry."

"Me, too," he said sincerely, pushing himself upright. He looked into the gift shop. "This is just the kind of place he would've come to. The museum, I mean. He kind of liked things like that." A wink, then. "He'd drive a hundred miles just to see someone's autographed picture of Elvis in the Kmart."

Maggie laughed quietly. "Well, like the sign says, we have odd, but we don't have Elvis."

He gestured. "You open?"

Another glance at Flower. "Couple of hours, maybe. I've got some things left to do for dinner." A sigh that added, *I don't know why I bother.* "So listen, if y'all want some lunch, better have it now while I'm in the mood."

He shrugged, looked to Flower, who shrugged back, and said, "Well, sure, why not. What's on the menu?"

"Remember that roast beef last night? Sandwiches. Some coleslaw, pickles, nothing fancy."

"Sounds good to me. And hey," he said, as she turned to leave, "do you mind if I use your phone? You can put it on my bill."

"Why Mr. Proctor," she said, fluttering her eyelashes outrageously, "I wouldn't have it any other way." A waggle of her fingers, and she was gone.

"Why, Mr. Proctor," Flower mimicked in a whisper, her eyes narrowed. Then she moved to his side. "Your office is open on Saturday?"

"This Saturday it is." He let the phone ring three times, hung up, and dialed again. When Lana answered, he said, "See if Gert's working today. Thursday night, Friday morning numbers if you can."

"What do you know yet?"

"Nothing."

"That's not acceptable."

"Tell me about it. Call when you know."

He sat at the end of the first table, facing the back. Flower sighed loudly onto the bench opposite, rested her elbows on the table and cupped her cheeks in her palms. Batted her eyelashes. Grinned like an idiot. And said in an eerie imitation of Maggie's voice, with an added gallon of thick Southern syrup, "Why, Mr. Proctor, sir, I thought only the official police were able to get phone records like that. You must be someone powerful important."

"Sometimes," he said, not responding to her joke, "I help people out, and they think they owe me. A little here, a little there."

"Boy," she said, abruptly impressed. "Must be some really interesting folks you know."

He shook his head, staring over her shoulder at the kitchen door barely seen in the shadows of the back. "Believe me, Flower, you do not want to know some of the people I know."

That clearly unsettled her, and her hands dropped into her lap. She began to gnaw gently on her lower lip, unsure what, if anything, she should say. He didn't like doing it, but whatever her reasons for sticking around, since this morning he had gotten the impression she had begun to think this was some kind of adventure. She didn't know Delany. She had seen a body, that was all. She had heard some stories. Now she probably thought he was after some kind of monster.

She was right.

But this monster was human.

He wasn't familiar with this part of the country, but he didn't doubt that it would be awfully easy to get lost in these mountains. Here, and in the Smokies, the Blue Ridge . . . someone familiar with the territory and familiar with the superstitions would be able, he suspected, to roam for quite a while without being seen, or getting caught. Doing what he wanted. Getting what he wanted.

What he didn't yet understand was why this sheriff, who obviously wasn't a dope despite his little good ol' boy game, had lied about Delany. He doubted it had anything to do with the elections; he knew, once they had met, that the man didn't think he was a fool.

So what purpose did it serve to spread the word that Delany had—

He started when Maggie set his plate in front of him, and told him if he needed anything else he'd have to holler because she'd be out back. When she left, Flower turned around and stuck out her tongue.

"You know," she said, eyeing her thick sandwich suspiciously, "there are some advantages to being a ghost." Then she reached over and touched his wrist. "Where were you?"

"Delany," was all he said, more brusquely than he'd intended.

They ate in silence for a while, avoiding each other's gazes. A muffled clatter from the kitchen the only noise inside; the return of the wind the only sound outside.

Until the front door opened and Taz strode into the lobby, his hair blown wild, his cheeks flushed.

"Figures," he said when he saw them. "When you weren't at the diner, I had a feeling." He blew into his hands. "That diner's like a morgue, you know? Weird people. One guy had a marble for an eye, I swear to God, no kidding." He blew on his hands again, rubbed them hard against his side. "And those damn clouds are coming back. I swear it looks like snow out there."

Proctor started to apologize, to explain, but was interrupted when the telephone rang. When Maggie didn't come out to answer it, or pick up from somewhere else in the building. Taz looked to Proctor, shrugged, leaned over the counter, and picked it up.

"Cumberland Motel and Museum, how may I help you?" He winked at Proctor as he listened. "She's not available at the moment. May I pass her a message?" The grin snapped off. "Tazaretti, Sheriff. I'm with Mr. Proctor, remember?" He nodded. "Sure. I'll tell her right away, thanks."

He hung up and puffed his cheeks, one finger tapping lightly against his chest.

"What?" Proctor asked.

"I'm supposed to tell her to be careful. There's been another one."

Immediately, Proctor was on his feet. He told Flower to stay where she was, pass the message on if she could find Maggie, and grabbed his coat. Taz already had the door open, and they ran for the car and were on the highway before he had his coat on.

"A man called Emil Vickers," Taz said from the passenger seat. "A place called Ridge Road."

Proctor nodded grimly, not bothering with the speed limit, not caring that Taz had braced his feet on the floorboard as if working a spare set of brakes. He wanted to get there before the body was moved.

He had to *see*.

He eased up only when he reached the first intersection, cursed at the street sign, and drove on, slipping on his sunglasses as he did. Although the light was still sharply bright, large clouds had begun to lumber over the eastern peaks. The shadow of one darkened the far bank; the shadow of another crawled over the rooftops. If it wasn't going to snow, the rain would be brutal.

"Nope," Taz said when they reached the second cross-street.

"We'll stop at a gas station," Proctor said, then changed his mind when he heard an ambulance siren and, a second later, saw one speed off the bridge and turn up the next street ahead.

"This is where I was," Taz said, holding on as Proctor whipped around the corner. "That," and he pointed, "is the library."

"Tell me."

Ten years ago, as best he could tell, everything was fine. Which is to say, normal. The usual hunting accidents, falls, an occasional hiker or hunter gone missing. To be expected in areas like this; the mountains are beautiful, but unless you know what you're doing, they're not always friendly.

Six years ago, however, the tone of the letters column began to change. As people turned up missing, or dead, the editorials condemned carelessness and ignorance as the cause of it all, much more strongly than before. And the letters . . . at least one or two every time which said, in effect, "Everybody knows what's really going on and why isn't somebody doing something about it?" Creatures loosed from the deepest shafts of the mine; forest creatures disturbed as civilization pushed deeper into the mountains; ancient curses, Indian curses, and at least one Gypsy curse.

Town officials and the sheriff scoffed, poked polite fun, and did everything but whip the letter-writers in public.

It didn't seem to make a difference.

"How many?" Proctor asked.

"Sixteen, counting Delany."

"What? That's nearly three a year, for God's sake."

Taz agreed, but as they followed the ambulance through a residential area, he pointed out that the average wasn't all that high, all things considered. It just seems that way when people blame it on monsters.

Besides, he added, they were all stretched out over the year, seldom more than one in a season, never more than one at a time.

"No mention of a possible serial killer?"

"Nope. Nothing. It's just like anyplace else—details are held back because the bodies that were found were in too gruesome a condition."

Or, they both knew without saying, because the police needed to hold back something so they could more easily dismiss the crank-call confessions.

The houses, most of them well kept, were a stark contrast to the melancholy face the main street wore. Hedges, fences, mowed lawns, children's playthings, wash on a line. A man hurrying east along the sidewalk with three hounds straining on a triple leash. One man standing on his porch, rifle crooked over one arm, talking with another man, who held a beer can in one hand and a shotgun in the other. An old man kneeling by his rose garden, covering each plant with a burlap bag. A young woman with a baby carriage, practically running around a corner.

The road began a slow curve to the north, and the homes fell away. A farm on one side, an empty pasture on the other, a small stand of trees in the center, darker against the sky as the clouds began to mass.

Proctor slowed when he saw the police car parked on the side of the road. Half a dozen men stood by a split-rail fence, looking into a field equal parts bare earth and grass. The ambulance pulled up behind the cruiser. Proctor pulled over and turned around to face townward. Once they were out, he waited for a moment, taking a series of deep breaths to get him used to the afternoon's chill.

Then he crossed the road to the corner of the fence, and looked at the dark form lying several yards away.

"Jeez," Taz said. "That's the old man from the bus stop."

Flower glared at the remains of her lunch, unsure whether to scream with anger or just leave, get in her car, and go home. First she's a chauffeur, now she's a messenger girl. And he didn't even ask if she wanted to go along. She huffed, picked up the sandwich and took an angry bite. As she chewed she stared at the curtains, watching them glow faintly with sunlight, fade as clouds scudded across the valley.

Messenger girl.

Well, that bitch will just have to wait until she was done, that's all there is to it. The way she'd been treated around here, Proctor was lucky she'd do it at all.

She took her time.

When she finished, she stretched her arms over her head until her shoulders popped. Then she squinted at her watch, cursed the woman for leaving it so dark in here, and said, "Oh, my, will you look at the time?" And laughed as she stood.

Taking her time, she went to the swinging kitchen door, pushed it open, and saw no one inside. The smell of cooking meat, baking bread, but no one there to watch over it. A small TV set on a counter, a silent baseball game in progress. With a frown, she wandered back to the lobby and finally, reluctantly, called Maggie's name.

No answer.

She called again, and walked into the gift shop. Another call, this one considerably less forceful than the others, as she checked the shelves and display cases, not really seeing anything, not really caring. Deliberately ignoring the pale neon sign that marked the museum's entrance until she couldn't stand it any longer and walked over.

The sliding glass doors were open.

She looked over her shoulder. "Maggie?"

She had never been inside, never had the desire. It was tempting, though. Quiet, a soft glow at the back, no overhead or wall lights, just the lights in all the cases.

She could hear the wind; she could hear her own breathing.

She stepped over the threshold and rolled her shoulders against the chill inside.

And behind her, a whisper: "You won't believe what I have in here."

TWENTY

Proctor moved cautiously along the fence, not wanting to get too close to the men clustered at the center. A few of them eyed him suspiciously, and he saw Dr. Murloch shaking his head as he kicked at the ground. A photographer leaned halfway over the fence, working a zoom lens and complaining about the angle.

And he saw what they did:

A small form lying on its side, dirt-smeared topcoat open, right arm hanging down its back, left arm on the ground in a shredded sleeve. Its face was turned toward the sky, wisps of grey hair stiffened by the wind. A partially crushed hat lay under its hip.

When a cloud-shadow passed over it, it seemed to blend into the ground; when the sun broke through, everything was too bright.

Including all the blood.

"Hey!"

He leaned against the fence and waited for the sheriff to stomp over, glowering, muttering, snapping orders to the ambulance attendants to hold their horses, they'd get what they wanted in a goddamn minute.

"What the hell are you doing here?"

Proctor looked at him blandly. "Hit-and-run, Sheriff Nathan?"

Nathan reared back, eyes narrowed. He lifted a heavy hand and jabbed an angry finger at the air in front of Proctor's chest. "You just get outta here, you hear? This isn't any of your concern."

"Oh, yes, it is," Proctor answered, and looked out at the body. "Emil Vickers, huh? Same man whose wife was murdered about four years ago, found her body caught under the bridge?"

Nathan sputtered. "That was an accident, Proctor. This"—and he waved sharply at the old man's body—"was a bear attack, pure and simple. You happy now? So git!"

Proctor slipped past him, one hand gliding along the top rail as he estimated the distance between the fence and the body. The sheriff grabbed for his shoulder, but he eased it away before contact was made. A glint made him look down, and he saw in trampled weeds a pair of wire-rimmed glasses. he didn't pick them up; he only pointed.

"Vickers?"

The sheriff, bluster abruptly gone, knelt, pulled a pen from his breast pocket, and poked at them. "Yeah, looks like it."

"No bear, Sheriff."

Nathan glared up at him. "You're from the city. What the hell do you know about bears?"

Proctor nodded toward the body. "I know that it rained like hell last night, Sheriff. I know that a bear, or a mountain lion, or whatever other critters you have in these mountains, unless it has wings, doesn't attack a man here, let him get away, climb over the fence after him, and kill him over there."

Nathan stood and backed away, looking at him sideways.

"No prints, Sheriff. No prints in the mud."

Nathan waited.

"He was thrown."

The sheriff started to laugh, stopped, and shook his head at the theories amateurs came up with when they didn't know the truth when it kicked them in the face. He sniffed and rubbed his nose. He looked back at the others with a tolerant half smile, and sniffed again. "Well, that's kind of interesting, Mr. Proctor, very interesting. But if, as you say, he was killed here, where, may I ask, is all the blood?"

Proctor pointed at a few drops near the man's right foot. "There." He stepped onto the blacktop and pointed again as the sheriff followed. "There." Pointed to a large dark smear caused by passing tires. "There." To a small viscous puddle in the center of the right-hand lane. "There." He hunched his shoulders against a gust and scanned the belt of low grass that led to the first line of trees.

And pointed without saying a word.

Nathan joined him, carefully skirting the blood trail, a hand in his coat pocket. He seemed thoughtful, and his animosity had faded, leaving behind a curious blend of suspicion and not quite fear. Proctor saw the men watching him, saw Taz leaning back against the fence, arms folded, waiting.

"Not much blood," Nathan finally said. "For a man running from his attacker."

"I don't think he ran. I think he was carried."

Nathan snorted. "Yeah, right. Guy kills him in the trees, carries him across the road, and tosses him—what? fifty feet?—into a field where anybody could see him. That about it?"

"Maybe he doesn't care. Maybe he wanted the body to be found."

"Oh, sure. Why?" The sheriff feigned intense interest. "In case you have a theory about that too."

The wind stopped, and the clouds began to merge.

Proctor stared at his shoes for several seconds, looked up without raising his head and said, "To scare you."

Nathan grunted.

"To remind you he's still around."

Nathan rolled his eyes.

"Listen," Proctor said, waving Taz to the car. "I don't know what you know, but I can guess that you're piling up those accidents reports so the people you're supposed to protect don't panic. That's a good thing, I guess. Understandable, anyway. The problem is, Sheriff, in case you hadn't noticed, they're already scared to death, and your games are only making it worse." He checked the sky, looked past Nathan to be sure the men had stayed where they were. "And if some of those deaths really were from accidental shootings, did it happen because the shooters thought they were after something else?"

He didn't expect an answer; he didn't get one save for a twitch at the corner of Nathan's left eye.

A crow landed on Vickers' shoulder, its head cocked, its beak slightly open. A deputy yelled at it, then picked up a stone and whipped it, high and wide. The bird spread its wings and backed up a step.

The photographer took a picture.

When Proctor looked up, he saw four more. Circling. Calling softly to each other. Taking their time.

The deputy threw another stone, this one bouncing off the old man's hip. The crow took off and joined the others.

Circling.

Taking their time.

Calling softly to each other.

"Look, Sheriff," Proctor said, rubbing a finger against the side of his nose, "I know you've got a crime scene to secure here, so I'll get out of your hair. Just let me know when you feel like talking, okay?" He started to walk away, turned and walked backward a few steps. "Sloan Delany was my friend, Sheriff. Don't wait too long."

He turned and headed for the car, listening to the crows, listening to the men mutter among themselves. Down the road, by the last house, he could see a group of people standing off to one side. Too far for details, but he had a suspicion most of them carried guns.

"Hey."

He looked back.

Nathan glanced uneasily at the others, then leaned forward as if that would make it more difficult for his men to see or overhear. *The museum,* he mouthed, waited until Proctor nodded that he understood, then whirled and began to yell. Snapping orders. Waving his hands. Wondering where in hell the crime scene tape was. He didn't look back once.

Proctor didn't run, but as soon as he was back behind the wheel, he groaned and said, "God damn, Taz," and shot away from the shoulder. "Flower. We left Flower back there."

Once things got moving, Nathan reached into his cruiser and grabbed a cell phone from the front seat. He punched the number in so hard, so rapidly, he had to cut himself off twice before he got it right.

Nobody answered.

"Cory," the doc called impatiently, "I gotta look at the body!"

"When I'm ready," he yelled back. "Nobody goes in there until I'm ready."

He tried again, and again there was no answer.

"Sheriff!"

Jesus, he thought, and threw the phone back into the car.

One man.

One man comes in, takes one damn look, and it all falls apart.

He strode toward his men, nodding impatiently when the photographer indicated that he had to go with him to make the visual record.

One man; and Nathan decided he didn't give a damn anymore. He probably wasn't going to get re-elected, they probably wouldn't even let him stay in town anymore. He didn't care. As long as it finally ended, he just did not care.

The crows circled.

A handful of raindrops splattered on what was left of the old man's cheek.

*   *   *

Dewey Plowman lived in a small, three-room house a little more than a mile from the Cumberland Motel. He had been born here, his mother had died here, his sister had run away from here when she was seventeen. There was too much distance and too many trees for him to see his neighbors, even after all the leaves had fallen; and behind was the wooded slope of Spooner Mountain.

He stood at the back door, shifting his weight from foot to foot, humming to himself, staring so hard through the dust-streaked pane that the nearest boles began to shift and shimmer, as if they were getting ready to uproot themselves and come on in.

The euphoria was gone.

No sooner had he walked in the door than the telephone rang, a poker buddy of his, giving him the news, telling him a bunch of the guys were getting a hunting party together, did he want in?

He didn't.

He kicked the base of the door angrily.

Why the hell did it have to be old man Vickers? Why couldn't it have been one of a hundred stinking drunks, or some guy who whipped his wife for nothing better to do, or one of the jerks who still haunted the campgrounds?

Oh, no, that would be too easy.

No, it had to be somebody everybody either cared about or felt sorry for. A useless old coot not worth a nickel, and not even that sorry-ass sheriff would be able to stop them this time.

He kicked the door again.

He whirled, yanked open the refrigerator door,

and snatched another can of beer from the well-stocked top shelf. His third, maybe his fourth, and he was just getting started.

No fame. No wealth.

He chugged the can without taking a breath, tossed it over his shoulder, and watched the trees move.

Five minutes later he belched loudly, grimaced at the sour taste in his mouth, and grabbed another beer.

One chance, he figured; he had maybe one chance to pull this off. If there were enough of those idiots out there tonight, they might make it nervous, keep it on the move, and maybe, just maybe, it would hit one of his traps.

That it hadn't before didn't make no never mind to him.

This was his last chance.

So what the hell, screw it, he might as well get ready.

Nathan heard them before he saw them—voices raised in fearful anger, hounds baying, a loud and incoherent prayer for divine guidance.

He stood over the body while Doc Murloch checked it over, taking off his sunglasses when he realized the clouds had finally drained the sunlight from the air.

"You're not going to be able to stop them," Doc said without looking up. "Not this time."

"Ain't even gonna try," he answered wearily. "I ain't even gonna try." He hitched up his belt when he saw them, fifteen at least, coming up the road.

"Oh hell, I might as well give it a shot anyway. Go through the motions so I don't get nailed later when one of them stupid bastards shoots another stupid bastard."

He started back for the fence, stopped, and said, "Tell me something, Doc."

"Sure."

"How did these people know about it so fast, huh? They were on their way before we even got here. Who the hell made the call?"

And the whisper said, *don't kill her . . . we're not ready yet.*

TWENTY-ONE

"Boss, what's the hurry?"

Proctor didn't know.

It was a feeling, nothing more. A niggling of urgency that made him impatient when he had to slow down for a large group of men heading toward the field. He saw guns, a pair of bloodhounds, and expressions that weren't going to take Sheriff Nathan's stories anymore.

They glared as he crawled through them, those in the center only reluctantly giving way. One raised a hand as if to try to stop him; another slapped the hood contemptuously with a hard open palm. A third pressed his face close to the driver's window, studying him until he turned his head and stared. The man backed off, stumbling in his haste.

"Lynch mob," Taz muttered.

Not so far from the truth, Proctor thought.

"If they had torches," Taz added, "it'd be like one of those old movies."

Proctor grunted. "Yeah. I guess so."

Once the mob was behind them, he accelerated to the speed limit and held the car there, one finger tapping the steering wheel, his left foot tapping the floorboard.

"Boss?"

"Proctor."

"Yeah. There's something I forgot to tell you before."

"Which is?"

"One of those missing people? A couple of years ago? It was a private investigator. Some guy from Michigan. They did a search and everything, but never found him."

People like you, Nathan had said.

Proctor nodded thoughtfully, but none of it yet made much sense. And when he told Taz what he had said to the sheriff, Taz wanted to know, with a nervous laugh, if he was kidding. The old man wasn't much, but he was deadweight. How big and how strong did you have to be to toss someone like that?

Not much sense at all.

The traffic light stopped them at the main street intersection. The bus stop was empty. A reclaimed army deuce-and-a-half chugged south, its bed loaded with dead furniture and tires, a warning flag flapping from the end of a pole that stuck out a good eight feet over the wire-bound gate. He checked the rear-view mirror; there was nothing behind him. No one on the sidewalks.

A splatter of rain on the windshield.

The streetlamps were on.

"Boss," Taz said when the light turned, "what are we talking about here?"

"I don't know," he answered truthfully. "Nathan told me to check the museum. I assume that's the one at the motel."

"A clue?"

"I don't know."

It didn't take long to catch up with the truck, and he hung back several lengths because he didn't want a sudden braking to put that pole through the windshield. From this angle it looked like a knight's lance ready for a charge.

"Taz," he said, "do you believe in ghosts?"

That wasn't what he was asking, and Taz knew it.

Two years ago he would have laughed, made some fun, pretended to look for the bottle of booze, or held up his fingers in a hasty cross to ward off the evil vampire; two years ago he would have seriously considered a new line of work because the question had been asked without a trace of irony.

Two years ago he sat in on one of Proctor's late-night sessions, listening to the others go over some cases his boss was about to handle on his own, as he always did. There were ghosts there, and other things, and he had listened with his mouth open, incredulous that so-called grown-ups could be taking such things so seriously. He knew from the start that these cases were scams and delusions; once the session was over, he had doubted they felt the same.

He would never admit it to anyone, but they, and the cases, had frightened him.

Guns were real; ghosts were not.

Shivs were real; movie monsters were not.

His ladies were real, the sex was real, his Jeep was real, the old neighborhood was real; things that went bump in the night were not.

His grandmothers talked to their dead husbands

all the time; that was real, and sometimes funny, and sometimes embarrassing. His grandfathers, they claimed, sometimes talked back, and that wasn't funny, and it was not real.

Delany was dead, and it wasn't a hit-and-run; that was real.

He watched the truck jounce, watched some of the tires bounce and threaten to roll off. He watched Proctor lose patience and begin to sway over the center line, looking for space to pass. He watched the clouds become smooth and darker, and watched the river turn black with no light to reflect.

Proctor wanted him to be honest, and so he said, "I don't know."

Proctor stomped on the accelerator, felt the car hesitate a split second before flowing out of its lane and sweeping around the truck. The driver honked at him several times, letting him know what an idiot he was because the last traffic light in town was going to stop them anyway.

He didn't care.

He stopped, fairly bouncing with impatience, and refused to look back when the truck sounded its horn again.

What he did care about was Taz's answer. He felt sure the kid was telling the truth, although there was, there had to be, a definite lean toward asking *are you sure you're not out of your mind*? A good thing. If it came down to it, an attitude like that would help keep him alive.

The light changed.

The car surged.

The wipers smeared another spray of rain across the glass.

"You know," Taz said tightly, a hand braced against the dashboard, "if I'm going to be a ghost, I sure don't want to haunt this place forever."

Proctor didn't slow down, not until he reached the motel entrance, and even then it was even money that he'd skid over the gravel and into the nearest tree. "Perfect," he said to the pale-faced kid when they stopped in the parking lot. He got out, grimaced at the slap a gust of damp wind gave him, and did his best not to run for the stairs.

The urgency had returned.

His instincts were not infallible, had often gotten him into more trouble than he would have normally if he'd only stopped to think, but he trusted them anyway. When he opened the door and stepped into the lobby, he didn't call out.

He listened.

The dining room was dark, the tables revealed in the lobby light's glow clear and clean.

The registration area was empty.

The closing door, their footsteps, the slow creak of a beam overhead were the only sounds.

No voices, near or distant.

Taz drifted immediately into the gift shop, moving to his right while keeping a wary eye on the museum's darkened entrance. Proctor followed, frowning when he couldn't see much through the open glass doors. He suspected he already knew the kinds of things that were in there, and couldn't imagine why Nathan had told him to check it out. One more thing that didn't make much sense.

Then Taz inhaled sharply and rapped Proctor's arm with a loose fist.

What? he mouthed.

On a shelf on the side wall, at eye level, were carved figurines of men in coonskin caps and women in frontier dresses, a rearing bear and a baying hound, a flatbed river barge with a family aboard, a flintlock rifle, a tomahawk, a long-stemmed clay pipe.

Made, a small hand-lettered sign announced, by local artisans, just as Maggie had told them.

He didn't get it.

Scowling, Taz rapped him again and pointed to the shelf below.

Ceramic and painted-glass figures, larger than the wooden carvings. Not beautiful but not bad, with another hand-lettered sign that proclaimed them products of local handicraft groups. Maidens in hoop dresses, gentlemen in waistcoats and top hats, children on swings, lovers beneath a magnolia tree, a Confederate soldier by a campfire, a dying Union soldier in the arms of a nurse, a racehorse in full gallop, a godawful Tennessee walker with a black jockey in front and a thermometer in its belly.

Proctor wanted to pick the walker up; but he couldn't move his arm.

He looked at the shelf below that; he looked in the nearest display cases; he looked back at the walker and knew exactly where Delany would have put it.

He still couldn't touch it.

Taz did. He picked it up and turned it over, then turned the base toward him.

Made in Lexington.

"Space vampire," Taz said. "He was here."

Proctor started for the museum, stopped, and headed quickly for the lobby. "Flower," he said when Taz asked; the museum, for now, could wait.

It didn't take long to make a quick search.

The dining room was too large and open, with only the kitchen door for another exit. The kitchen itself was empty, but Taz checked the larger cupboards and storage spaces anyway, while Proctor glanced into a walk-in refrigerator and saw nothing but shelves, and a slab of hanging meat. A small storage room was the source for fresh linens and cleaning equipment. Through the rear door were two steps down to a strip of worn grass, and the gravel drive that led from the side parking lot to the parking area behind the cabins. The woods were less than thirty feet away, and going in there now, without protection or help, was out of the question.

Nothing behind or under the counter.

No one in the tiny office in back of the counter.

Taz ran outside to check her cabin while Proctor made another pass, looking for a door or a stairway that would led to a higher, or lower, level. He didn't find one; nor was he able to find any hint of where Maggie Medford had gone. Her office, when he checked again, was unremarkable. Ledgers, a computer, a file cabinet with business folders, and nothing else. A narrow door led from there to the kitchen.

No obvious trapdoor to a cellar, or even a crawl space; no obvious ceiling trap to an attic.

He called out several times, as much hoping for a

response as to break the silence that dogged him. That made it worse. His voice didn't echo, but it wasn't swallowed by all the wood. It traveled, sounding distant, as if he were calling from somewhere else.

By the time he returned to the front door, he was concerned about Maggie as well. Why would she leave without hanging out a "be back later" sign on the door? Something like that.

Frowning, he stepped outside, gasping a little at the chill the afternoon had taken on with the death of the sun. Taz yelled from the walk in front of Flower's cabin, beckoning urgently.

He ran.

"Car's gone," Taz said. "Clothes are gone. The door's unlocked, though, in case you want to look around."

He did.

The interior was the same, with the same faintly musty smell. The closet and all the drawers were empty, and nothing had been left in either the bathroom or the kitchenette. Not that he expected to find anything. He had treated the woman badly. As upset as she had been, she had volunteered to help him out, drive him around, and when he left her in the dining room, it had been with a curt order to pass on a message to a woman she despised, and who couldn't stand her. No good-bye. Not even a thank-you.

Jesus, you're an idiot, he thought as he slammed the door behind him.

"Boss," Taz said, "I think you pissed her off."

He grunted, felt a raindrop hit the back of his neck,

and sighed. Then he tossed the car keys to Taz and told him to get on the road, ride south for at least ten miles, to see if he couldn't catch up to her. If not, check to see if there was anyone at the Kave, just in case she stopped in on her way home.

"Boss—"

"Proctor, damnit."

"Yeah. But I don't get it. I mean, you and her weren't exactly—"

"Did it ever occur to you that she might not have left on her own?"

Taz opened his mouth, closed it, said, "Oh," and added, "Covering the bases, right?"

"Right. Now go, before she gets halfway to Nashville, for crying out loud."

"What about you?"

He looked at the motel.

He didn't have to answer.

TWENTY-TWO

He stood on the museum's threshold and braced himself.

A long time ago, at the time of the first winter dream, he had done a similar thing, standing alone at a doorway, chilled inside and out, wanting to go through and lacking the nerve. What was beyond, if he was right, would contradict just about everything he had believed in. The world would keep revolving and the stars would remain cold, but nothing else would be the same.

Ever.

And it hadn't been.

. . . *a cold night in December, and just enough snow to cover the grass.*

A full moon.

A strong wind.

And a man standing on the lawn, just at the edge of the kitchen-window light.

The rest of the house is dark.

Proctor stands at the dining-room window. Staring. Not believing.

The man wears a camel's hair topcoat, unbuttoned, col-

lar up, his hands in the pockets. His sparse white hair rises and twists, and falls with the wind. His cheeks are full, the cold giving them color. Stray snowflakes dance around him, but not one of them lands.

Proctor rubs his face hard, rubs his eyes until they hurt, leans as close to the pane as he can get.

Then the man on the lawn looks up, and Proctor blinks, shakes his head, and races for the kitchen door.

And stands there, afraid to open it, feeling the draft around his ankles, feeling the cold.

A dream, he thinks; nothing but a dream.

Nevertheless he opens the door and goes outside, and the man on the lawn smiles ruefully at him, snow on his shoulders, snow in his hair.

Proctor walks slowly across the grass, blinking at the flakes that dance around his eyes, stopping a few feet away when he realizes that the only footprints in the snow are his own.

Dad? he whispers, terrified and pleased at the same time.

Hello, Ethan, his father answers . . .

. . . just before he vanishes, leaving Proctor out there alone, standing in the snow, shivering violently, weeping silently.

Not a dream at all.

Now, in this place of silence and lights that made shadows out of shadows, it wasn't so much the possible discovery to be made that caused him to hesitate, but the fact that, if he did make it, he wouldn't completely disbelieve.

The stuff of dreams, the soul of nightmares.

There was, for him, always a moment like this,

when he had to ask himself if he really wanted to know. And if, in the knowing, he would wish he never had.

Since the time of the winter dream, there had been both.

Since the time of the winter dream, he had only once failed to take the step.

Now, in this place of silence, he knew full well he was stalling.

Delany was dead.

He had no choice.

He stepped in.

Automatically he sidled right and his hand went out to slap at the wall, looking for a switch to give him something more to see by. Finding none there, he tried again on the left, and failed.

He wasn't surprised. Any more than what was here would have been wrong.

No illumination then but the pale white trapped in the cases, and the tall cylinder of light at the back of the room.

And the silence.

Just a step behind him it was quiet with the quiet creaks of beams and planks and the sough of the still slow wind; but here, one step over, there was nothing but the light, and the dark, and no sounds at all.

One look at the displays under glass, and he knew they weren't what the sheriff wanted him to see. Interesting stuff, some of it, and probably some of it might even be genuine. But Andy Jackson and Daniel Boone had nothing to do with nearly a score of brutal murders.

He moved warily toward the back, aware that the silence was causing him to remain as quiet as possible. Barely lifting his feet. Keeping his breathing shallow. Letting his arms hang away from his sides so they wouldn't brush against the hang of the denim jacket.

That was okay with him; a sudden noise now would probably stop his heart. And to think, just a day or so ago, he was complaining about being bored.

Glancing left and right, grunting softly now and then when he spotted something he might otherwise have examined more closely, he made his way to the end of the center aisle and checked behind him quickly before facing the cylinder. Seven feet high, he estimated, maybe a little less.

The bubbles rose bottom to top, big and small, lit from below, giving them depth.

After a moment's search he found the card at the rounded base, but he couldn't read it, not even when he leaned over to peer at it more closely. He would have to kneel; he wouldn't do it.

A finger touched the glass surprisingly cold.

He watched the bubbles, followed their journey, and looked away quickly before they took him in and prevented him from seeing clearly the shadowy figure their movement veiled.

A clever manipulation; the eye wants to see it but the eye also wants to watch the bubbles.

The bubbles, big and small and forever rising, would win every time, and the details of the other that the watcher took away would be the details he filled in afterward, not the details that were there.

As he looked again, concentrating on the winking gaps between the rising bubbles, he felt the room become smaller; something new had been added.

The creak of leather, the hush of cloth against cloth.

A tentative approach, not a stealthy one.

He waited.

While the bubbles rose.

He glanced to his left, did not smile, did not frown, reached out and touched the cylinder again. "Thick glass," he said, and this time he did smile when he realized he had whispered.

The bubbles again, and the lighting, and the silence.

"It killed her husband," said Cory Nathan, whispering himself. A church whisper, for fear that God would overhear and strike him down. "So she says."

Shadows of bubbles sliding upward across his face.

All you have to do, the sheriff said, is close your eyes at night, and you can hear them.

Someone will tell you, don't worry, it's only an owl out there, a nighthawk, maybe a bat, maybe just the wind settling in the trees. It's a cat stalking a nest, a raccoon or skunk rooting for garbage, Neighbor Jones out walking his dog or just out walking on account of he can't get any sleep. It's a car passing, its muffler not working right. It's snow sliding off the roof. It's a branch against the window. It's leaves in the gutter or scooting across the yard.

It's the house settling, boards expanding or contracting; the house talking to itself.

It's the wind across the mouth of the chimney.

A loose shutter, maybe, or the top of a plastic trash can spinning down the street.

There's always an explanation, and it's certain to sound reasonable because what else could it be?

A while back, a year or two, one of those private eye fellas has me in my office, we're practically nose to nose, and I swear he's so red in the face I thought he'd drop dead right on my floor. He's telling me his client's husband comes all the way down here for a little hunting, he goes into the mountains and he doesn't come back, and what the hell am I doing about it? I tell him the truth. I tell him that the first thing is, there's no telling how many hunters and fishermen and campers there are in there because they're not required to check in with me before they go. The smart ones do. They ask about the places to stay away from, the most popular, the ones where they won't run into anyone else. The others, they just go. Like this guy. I never saw him, I never knew he was there until his wife calls me. Then I make sure she's sure this is where he came, and we go have a look. The whole nine yards, hounds and men and all.

Nothing.

This guy says we're incompetent, we don't have the right equipment, we don't give a damn if it ain't one of ours.

About an hour later he demands the name of the best man in town. Scout, he calls him. Jesus Christ, a scout. I give him a couple of names, he leaves, and I never saw him alive again.

I know what the papers say because they say what I give them. What I don't tell them is what they wouldn't print if I did.

There are places, Mr. Proctor, gullies and ditches and caves and hollers and little valleys where nothing but a creek can get through. Doc Murloch and I, we found them all in all those places. First we didn't say much, out of respect for the families; then we didn't say anything because we'd run out of ways to say a bear done it, or they fell, or they ran across some idiot living back there who takes offense at being disturbed.

Lies like that.

But they know, Mr. Proctor.

The people who live here know.

It ain't the wind, or a critter, or some guy walking his dog, or creaking boards or flapping shutters.

It's him.

It's always him.

Proctor watched the bubbles, and the shadow that stood behind them.

She says, Maggie does, that her husband saw something in a clearing up on the mountain out back, went up the next day to take a look, never came back. She went after him. She found him. Dead. Like Emil, like your friend.

Like the others I've found.

She never told me until weeks later, when I pressed her about Jack. Her husband, that is. And when I saw finally this here, she told me the rest. How she hunted it down and dragged it back on her own and built this glass thing and stuck it in and sealed it. Some kind of preservative, I figure, though I never have been able to smell it.

You ever get a good look at that card down there, without you going blind, it says *Genesis*.

I asked her why, because it's kind of blasphemous, coming from the Bible and all, and she says it's because it's only the beginning.

I didn't get it, she didn't explain.

I thought about it a while, finally figured she meant because there were more of them out there, maybe a family of them or something, and they'd get their revenge, or she would, or both.

Anyway, I didn't push it, and I didn't fight it. Maggie's a strong woman in more ways than one. When she goes off the deep end, like with this here, I just back off and give her room. The only thing I can do.

I mean, look at it, Proctor. Can't see much, of course, the water and them damn bubbles and the way the light is and all, but take a look. If you kind of jog around, look between, it looks almost human, don't it? Don't know if those patches are hair or fur. Face sort of pushed out a little like that, the eyes way back, sometimes I think it's some kind of dog, the kind with the mugs that look mashed in. Once in a while I think I see teeth. My momma used to say fingers like that are piano-player fingers, but best I can tell there ain't any long nails. I sure don't see any claws.

Hard to tell, what with the light and the bubbles.

The thing of it is, Mr. Proctor, you know this thing here can't be real. Wax, rubber, something, I don't know. But it ain't real. Never existed, and neither do its kin.

If you want to know what I think, what killed those people, I think it's Maggie.

*   *   *

Proctor watched the bubbles, and knew that much of what the man said had been the truth.

Explain the little noises, the half-heard sounds, the bits of shadow shifting just behind the shadows, and you don't have to worry about what's out there, in the night. Nothing to fear; it's just the wind.

A touch of cold air tickled his cheek.

He brushed at it unconsciously, and felt the room change again.

He looked over his shoulder just as the sheriff did, and they grinned sheepishly at each other when no one was there.

"Spooked me," he admitted.

"Spooked myself," the sheriff answered, rolled one shoulder, pulled at his belt. "It's this place."

They still whispered, and that made their grins return, broader, without embarrassment this time.

"Why Maggie?" he wondered, making it clear at the same time he felt considerable doubt.

Nathan shrugged. "You didn't know her before Jack. During Jack, even. When he died, she changed." A look on his face—despair, and something else—as a finger tapped his temple; "just a little, you know what I mean?"

He did, but he didn't agree. "Sheriff, no offense, but she couldn't have thrown that old man. Not like that."

"I'm open. Who?"

Proctor looked back at the cylinder.

The shadow opened its eyes.

TWENTY-THREE

Taz clocked ten miles, then added another ten for good measure before he decided he would have to have Blaine's jet to catch up with Flower now, and he'd really been pushing it as it was. Still, he wasn't all that heartbroken. Next on the list was the Kat Kave, which he decided had to be one of the perks of the job.

He was pretty sure, though, that he wouldn't find her there, either. She was gone. Proctor had pissed her off royally, and she was gone for good.

Sounded like one of the songs he'd had on the radio a while ago. He'd surfed the dial during the first couple of miles, and found nothing but Saturday preachers and country music, neither of which he could stand to listen to for more than a few minutes at a time. Everything else was static.

He hummed a little, sang a little, couldn't stop himself from watching the river roll by in the other direction. This was, all in all, a pretty nice car, but he missed his old Jeep. This was soft, that was hard-riding; this was comfortable, that had the comfort of a soft brick; that growled and snarled and felt like it was going to fall apart underneath him every time he stepped on the gas; this was smooth, and it was quiet, and he had had enough of quiet for one day, thanks.

Cumberland Motel. Bates Motel. Six of one, as his father used to say.

Which reminded him of Delany, and the old man lying all broken in the field, and suddenly his left hand jabbed the button that slid his window down. The road-wind shoved at him, and filled his ears with its voice, and he didn't mind at all that it felt like midwinter. The shock gave him something else to think about besides the bile that was ready to leave his stomach in a hurry.

This absolutely, positively was not what he had signed up for.

Bodies and blood were in books about private eyes; unspoken stories about things that lived in the woods and caused those bodies and blood belonged in the movies.

In the tunnel he didn't honk the horn; he just wanted to get to the other side.

When he did, the clouds were ready—a drizzle just heavy enough to make him turn on the wipers and, for good measure, the headlamps as well. When his teeth began to chatter, he closed the window and tried the radio again. Mostly static now, the voices he did hear like ghosts in a high wind.

"Jesus," he muttered, and shut it off, shook his head sharply, and reminded himself that Proctor was used to these kinds of cases. Scams and tricks, people hiding behind masks. Not, he thought sourly, that it made them any easier to take.

He passed the motel and almost stopped when he

saw the cruiser parked at the side. The sheriff decid-
ing to see if they had taken his advice, probably. He
grunted. Let the boss deal with the hick in John
Wayne clothes; he had a higher mission, and there it
was, with Paul Tazaretti written in neon all over it.

Two cars and a pickup were parked outside. He
pulled in beside the truck, checked his hair in the
rearview mirror, and got out. Took a breath for control, and hurried to the entrance.

It was larger than he'd expected.

He stood in a short hall, a cloakroom on his right
with a scrawny, wire-haired woman leaning on her
forearms on the half door's shelf. Granny glasses, tat-
toos around her wrist, a formless dress covered with
brightly colored flowers he was positive had never
existed in nature. A small-watt bulb hung uselessly
overhead, and directly in front of him was an obviously thick, obviously padded swinging door behind
which he could hear the raucous bass thud of music
he had never heard before. It was so pervasive he
could feel it through his soles.

"You thinking about going in?" the woman asked,
lighting a cigarette twice as long as her longest
finger.

Big-city suave deserted him instantly; he had never
been in a place like this before, didn't know the rules.

"Gonna be awfully boring if you're deaf," she said,
laughing through the smoke she blew at the opposite wall.

"No. Sorry. Yes, I mean." He reached for his wallet
when she told him there was a cover charge of ten
bucks, no Confederate funny money, no credit cards,
no checks, no traveler's checks, and no goddamn

pennies. "Actually," he said, "I'm looking for someone."

She shook her head sadly. "Life is like that, son. We're all looking for someone. Roy Orbison said it best, don't you think?" She frowned, blew more smoke. "At least I think it was him. Maybe it wasn't. Goddamn noise addles my brain sometimes."

This, he thought, is not the *Twilight Zone*, it's the damn *Outer Limits*.

"Miss Power," he blurted, holding on to his ten.

"Flower?" She looked at him closely. "You her son or what?"

"No," he answered indignantly. "I'm . . . my friend and I, that is, we met her last night, had lunch today, and I thought I'd stop by, see if she wanted dinner."

She looked at him closer still, making him squirm.

He pointed at the door. "Can I just . . ." He shrugged. "You know, poke my head in, see if she's there?"

"She ain't."

"Oh."

"Gone for the season."

"Oh. Yeah, right. She said that."

"She say that, why are you here?"

Great, he thought; maybe I should just go ahead and look. What's she going to do, leap over the door and tackle me, beat me senseless with that cigarette?

She shook her head wearily. "You know, son, I've seen that look more times than I care to remember." She held up the cigarette. "So let me tell you that there's a man on the other side, his name I swear to God is Wilford, he's got muscles on his damn muscles, and no brains to speak of. You go barging in there without one of these stupid tickets I hand out to all my customers, I'm afraid you're gonna be deader than Emil Vickers. Messier, too."

He smiled wanly.

The music stopped.

She approved of his decision; her eyes widened. "Say, you're one of those men, aren't you."

He didn't know what to say, so he nodded. "How'd you know?"

"This place may be spread out to hell and gone, honey, but you can't fart without some old biddy getting on the phone." She blew smoke, studied the tip of her cigarette. "Sorry about your friend."

"Thanks." He leaned a shoulder against the wall. "See, the thing is, Flower was kind of helping us—"

"No kidding?"

"No. Really."

The woman exhaled a nobody-tells-me-anything sigh, reached under the shelf and pulled out a small theater ticket. It would, she told him, get him through this door, and the next one. Just walk straight to the other side. Wilford would be along there somewhere. Show him the ticket, no dawdling, and go on through. Dressing room was the first door on the left. Maybe one of the girls has seen her today.

Taz thanked her.

"No sweat. Just put my name in the book." His look made her grin. "Don't you detective fellas always write books? About your cases? Well, you just put in my name, big, so I can read it."

"Sure," he said.

"Charity."

"I'm sorry?"

"My name is Charity. Charity Alcort." What was left of the cigarette pointed at his chest. "*Ms.* Charity Alcort, and one crack gets you Wilford."

He had no intention of making a crack, or saying anything else for that matter. He nodded, pushed through the heavy door and, with the ticket clearly visible in his left hand, walked straight across a large, dimly lit room toward the door he saw on the other side. A glance left showed him an empty horseshoe stage studded with a half dozen gleaming brass poles, and a dozen or more small round tables. Three men, tops, sat there. A bar on his right took up most of the wall, the female bartender dressed, to his surprise, like a bartender—white shirt, black slacks, black bow tie. She gave him a nod, he nodded back, and nearly stopped when the far wall came into focus.

Wilford wasn't tall, but Charity hadn't been exaggerating about the muscles. The man's arms were folded over his chest, bulging the biceps and accentuating the impossible expanse of his torso.

When the bouncer noticed him and glared, Taz hastily waved his ticket, praying the woman had given him the right one. Without expression, the man spread a monster palm on the door beside him and pushed it open.

Just in time for the scream.

Taz was quicker.

He raced through the open door into a hallway, and saw another open door at the back. He could see a porch on the other side and, as he approached it, a man dragging a struggling redhead toward the trees by one arm, keeping her so off-balance she couldn't twist herself free.

On the porch a tall blonde in a kaleidoscope kimono shrieked when he came through, but he didn't bother to slow down. He vaulted the railing, and the attacker immediately released the woman and made for the woods. He didn't get more than a dozen steps before Taz came up beside him, grabbed his hair in both hands, stopped, turned, and slammed him onto his back. Then he straddled him at the hips and showed him a fist.

"Don't," he ordered. Frowned as he realized it was the guy with the broom. Dewey, Flower had called him.

Dewey Plowman was in no condition to do much of anything. He gasped for a breath while holding the back of his head with both hands.

"I'll kill him," the redhead snarled, moving side to side like a boxer planning his next punch. "Stand aside, let me kill him."

"Help," Dewey gasped, tears of pain in his eyes.

"You okay?" Taz asked her.

The redhead sneered, looked at him for the first time, and blinked. "Who the hell are you?"

"Help," Dewey whispered. "Just wanted help."

The blonde shrieked hysterically again when Wilford exploded onto the porch and caught himself just before he splintered the railing and fell through. Charity was right behind him. She shut the blonde up with a sharp word, and called, "Grayleen, what the hell's going on?"

Grayleen was so mad she could barely speak, and

Taz hunkered down over the fallen man, grabbed his chin, and said, "Talk to me, Dewey."

Plowman blinked away his tears, shook his head, and gasped when Taz squeezed.

"Talk to me."

"I needed . . ." Dewey winced until Taz released his grip, shuddered when the hand moved from his chin to his chest to keep him pinned down. "Bait, you know? for the trap."

"Trap?" Grayleen yelled. "What trap?"

"We would've gotten rich," Dewey said to her, although he still looked at Taz. "Catch it, sell it, make millions."

"Catch what?" Taz said.

"Speak up!" Charity called. "And hurry it up, scum, it's raining out here!"

Dewey mumbled something Taz couldn't hear, pushed harder, and the man closed his eyes and said, "Genesis." Very softly.

Taz wanted to know what the guy was talking about, but a fuss made him look up just as Charity hustled her bouncer and the blonde inside, closed the door behind them, and moved back to the rail. When he looked at Grayleen, her rage had been replaced by openmouthed disbelief. He was also aware for the first time that she wore a fringed robe that barely reached her knees, that all she had on underneath was a G-string covered in rhinestones, and a bikini top. Such as it was.

Reminding himself what he was here for, Taz forced himself to look down at Plowman, and grabbed the man's shirt with both hands. "You sorry . . . let me get this straight. You were going to use this lady as bait to catch a killer?"

Plowman hesitated before nodding fearfully.

Taz straightened, and as he did, hauled the man easily to his feet. He didn't let go. "I think you and I, we're going to have a talk with the sheriff."

"I don't believe it," Grayleen whispered, her voice trembling. "My God, Dewey, what were you . . . ?" She stopped when she saw Taz looking, and tried to belt her robe, but her hands shook too much. One tear, then another, until she cried silently and trudged back to the porch, hands waving them all away, waving everything away.

Taz followed, not caring that Plowman had begun to complain that his arm hurt, take it easy.

He had just reached the porch steps, when he heard it.

"Oh Lord," Charity said.

Taz looked at the trees, and heard it again.

Nathan sat on the top step of the motel porch and looked at the highway. "I have never, and I mean never, been so scared shitless in my life." His laugh was nervous. "You saw it, right? Tell me you saw it so I don't have to jump into that river and let it take me."

Proctor, who wasn't feeling all that solid himself, pushed his hands back through his hair, wondering if that was Taz he had seen speeding by just as they'd left the building. "I saw it," he said. "I just don't believe it."

"Well, shit, neither do I. I just want to make sure you saw it too."

Proctor smiled at him. "It was the light, and those bubbles, and that damn story of yours."

Nathan nodded. "Thank God."

Proctor agreed, but something still bothered him, and it wasn't the scare he'd just gotten. They had both yelled, both jumped what must have been a dozen feet, and both felt like idiots when, upon checking, realized the eyes weren't open at all.

It hadn't taken long for them to leave the museum, not bothering to go through the ritual of making excuses to each other.

Once outside, however, he began to wonder. Something about that cylinder was curiously familiar, even though he had never seen anything like it before. As the sheriff muttered about having a word with Maggie, Proctor couldn't stop looking over his shoulder at the door.

What? he asked himself; what?

"I need a drink," Nathan declared, slapping his hands on his thighs. "I need to visit General Lee and get myself stinking."

Proctor looked at him.

"Bar," the man explained. "The General Lee is a bar."

And Proctor had it.

"Damn," he said, and used the sheriff's shoulder to brace him to his feet. With a "wait here," he hurried back to the museum.

A lounge. A hotel lounge in some town somewhere. The bar on one side of the room; on the other, booths and tables, separated from the bar by a ceiling-high partition—water between two thicknesses of opaque glass, with a curtain of bubbles rising from the bottom.

If he was right—

The front door slammed open and Nathan yelled, "Proctor, get out here. Now!"

One look was all he needed before he turned and ran to the porch.

And heard it.

"You're going to tell me that glass thing is empty, aren't you?" the sheriff said.

Proctor didn't have to nod.

He heard it again.

A long and slow cry, in the trees, in the rain.

Starting low, moving high.

Tailing off into silence.

For a very long time there was nothing left but the rain.

TWENTY-FOUR

Proctor sat at the cabin table.

Taz paced the length of the room from bathroom to front door. His jacket lay on the bed, there was a towel around his neck, and his left hand kept groping the air as if trying to snare the words he wanted.

Nathan was long gone. Got into his cruiser with just a look, not a word, and tore up the highway at speed. Taz had pulled in right after the sheriff had left, hair straggling, dripping, saying nothing but "I'm sorry," over and over as Proctor brought him to the cabin; he kept looking at the mountain.

A single light hanging over the table.

When Proctor leaned back, he slipped into shadow.

"Sit down," he said, not unkindly.

Taz stopped, but he didn't sit. "He got away. The son of a bitch got away. There was all this yelling and Plowman whining, then that . . . that awful noise, and we were so spooked he just got away, ran into the woods before I knew what was happening."

"Taz. Please sit down."

Taz flapped his arms against his sides. "Half-naked women all over the place. Well, two of them anyway.

One won't stop screaming, the other one wants blood." He looked to the walls, the ceiling, snapped the towel from around his neck and ran it over his hair. "If what we heard is what you saw in . . ." He swallowed, and suddenly dropped onto the edge of the bed, shaking his head, hands clasped between his knees. "Jesus, Proctor, what the hell is it?"

Proctor's hand reached into the light, picked up the telephone receiver, and dialed.

"Now what?" Taz complained.

Lana answered and Proctor asked her a question. Grunted. Said, "Not yet, but soon," and hung up. Taz, in the greylight that floated through the window, looked shaken, bloodless, ready to bolt. "You were right."

The kid didn't understand.

"You said, yesterday, he couldn't have called from inside if that noise was a car or truck. But he did. Because it wasn't. His call came from one of these cabins." He held up a hand to prevent comment. "Nathan told me a while ago that Maggie hasn't been right since her husband died. I'm guessing they were extremely close, devoted, and the loss left her not quite whole."

Taz's eyes widened. "You're saying *she's* that thing? Some kind of werewolf or something?"

"No."

He still didn't get it, by his expression and the desperate wave of a hand.

"One of two possibilities," Proctor told him, using a foot to drag his bag to his side. He reached into it. "She buried him on the mountain where she found him. A clearing, I'd guess. Maybe a favorite spot of theirs. Which turns the mountain—the whole mountain, Taz, and everything around it—into a shrine for him." He pulled out a handgun, and two magazines. "If Nathan's right, she might well have decided that no one, but no one, disturbs his rest."

"But that's crazy!"

"Yes. It is."

"What . . . you know, I really no kidding don't want to know, but . . . what's the second thing?"

Proctor smiled grimly as he slid one of the magazines into place, waiting until it was locked before he said, "That thing is real, Nathan's wishful thinking aside." Then he pointed, and waggled his fingers until Taz reached behind him, grabbed the denim jacket and tossed it over. He caught it with one hand, and opened it. "I hate those holster rigs, and you can't stick one of these things in your pocket or your belt. Damn barrel hurts unless you're built right, and I'm not. Doc has a friend who made this coat with a built-in." He shrugged, slipped the gun into its holster in the lining, and dropped the jacket onto the table.

"Jesus," Taz whispered.

"Which?" Proctor asked. "The gun or the thing?"

He didn't expect an answer, and he didn't get one. He felt sorry for the young man, realizing this was too far from his normal life with or without Black Oak. Bewilderment and uncertainty, and not a small amount of fear, had sent his mind off that definition of confusion, and the struggle to maintain control was evident on his face.

"Remember what I told Flower last night?" he said gently. "About knowing things."

The kid jerked a nod.

"No bull, Taz. It's true."

The wind gusted; rain slapped against the pane, and for a moment the greylight darkened.

"You don't have to believe me, and it's not my job, or my mission, to convince you. But the sheriff told me a story . . ."

. . . quiet sounds, night sounds, the way a shadow turns, the way a distant light burns, the way something along the roadside catches a headlight and glows; just a dog, just a cat.

. . . just the wind.

"One way or another, I have to find out which this one is. For Delany, because it's right. For me, because I have to. This time, I can't do it without your help. No options, Taz. No options."

Taz swallowed, blinked hard. "I . . . don't have a gun."

"With luck, I won't need this one. It doesn't matter. You're not leaving my side until this is all over."

Taz nodded doubtfully. "So why . . . why have the gun at all?"

Proctor grinned. "Because sometimes I'm dumb, but I'm definitely not stupid."

He stood and put on the jacket, slipping the extra magazine into another inside pocket. "Get your coat, we have to find Flower." He stood for a moment, watching the rain. "We'll start with the cabins. There's what, six? Eight? Then the main building. There has to be a cellar or an attic, we were too quick before, we missed it somehow."

They stepped outside; the rain was still light and steady.

Taz snapped up his collar, snapped his fingers once, and seemed to make up his mind. "No rules?"

Proctor nodded. "No rules. The door is locked, break a window or kick the sonofabitch in."

They started with the first cabin in line, did not exclude Taz's, and found nothing until they reached the last one, pushed into the trees that crowded the motel property.

Like the others, the door was locked and they battered it open.

Proctor went in first, stopped, and barely heard Taz moan, "Oh, God."

Dewey hadn't stopped running since he'd gotten away from that kid. Using his arms as shields, he bulled past trees and plowed through brush that didn't get out of his way.

There were six traps in all, but from the sound of it, he didn't think he'd have to bother with those higher up toward the summit. And since he couldn't be in all places at all times, he figured to take the nearest one, just a few hundred yards away, and plant himself.

If he was wrong, he was wrong. He didn't think it was going anywhere. They hadn't caught it yet.

If he was right, he was king, simple as that.

And he'd still share with Grayleen. He had no illusions; she couldn't stand the sight of him. But he was convinced the money would make all the difference between a cold winter's night, and one where she danced just for him.

He pressed a hand against his side, making sure the gun was still there. He wouldn't use it, wouldn't kill it, but he wasn't about to let himself be crow bait either.

Another tree to go around, and he stopped for a breather, swiping the rain from his beard, wrinkling his nose at the smell that rose from the wool of his coat. The money comes, first thing he'd do after Grayleen was get himself one of those new coats he'd seen on TV. Expensive as hell, waterproof like a duck, with its own hood and tons of pockets.

Heaven; easy heaven.

Easy now, he thought, stepping away from the tree; don't spend it, fool, before you got it.

His legs protested, but he moved on, not quite as fast but a whole lot more quietly. He wanted to be able to move when he got there. No Grayleen to lure it, he'd have to do that himself. He had to be able to move; he had to be able to jump.

The only thing he couldn't do was predict which way it would come.

Maggie sat on a boulder, hands clasped around her knees, huddled under a hooded poncho that covered her head to foot.

Far below she could get peeks at the motel roof when the wind shifted leaves and branches; she could hear an occasional sharp banging she soon figured out were the two men breaking into the cabins. That disappointed her. She had been hoping they would go through the main building first, driving themselves crazy looking for the slut. Still, it didn't make no never mind to her. They would find what they would find, then come after her for sure.

"Good," she said, rocking back and forth. "Good."

The boulder, six feet high and ridged with natural steps, sat in front of a grassy hump that extended out of the slope. Thickets all around it. Trees hovering above.

Unless you stepped around the boulder, you'd never see the mouth of Jack's cave.

They had discovered it years ago and had, giddy with love and a little brandy, proclaimed it their own. No bear ever used it, or anything else but an infrequent snake as far as they could tell. So they had cleaned it out, left sleeping bags and lamps inside, and when they got tired of the people and the work and the world, they climbed up, and in, and hid out for a while.

After he died, after sweet old Cory carried him down the mountain, she knew she would find him again, here.

"So will you," she said to the last banging she heard.

Her fingers tightened; she gnawed on the inside of her cheek until sharp pain stopped her.

She hadn't admitted it to Jack yet, but those two bothered her a little. Certainly more than anyone else ever had. Not the younger one so much, but the older man.

Proctor.

As soon as she had seen his eyes and heard his voice, she had known he should never get inside the museum.

He would see Jack.

And he would know.

She didn't understand why, but he would know.

A noise to her right, and she looked over quickly. "Jack?"

No; nothing but a fall of rain landing on a bush.

She was worried about him too. He had never called like that before. Silent she had found him, and silent he had remained, doing as he was bidden most of the time, once in a while striking out on his own just to have a little fun. Now he sensed something she didn't, she was sure of it.

He was loose on the mountain, and nothing she had been able to do all afternoon had brought him back to her.

Where he belonged.

Another noise; she didn't look.

He would come back to her when he came back to her, and nothing she could do would change that now. All she could do was wait, and hope, and pray for his safety.

Oh, *Lord*, how she missed him!

Helly, shivering even though it was actually too warm in the building, closed one eye and looked through the one-way peephole in the dressing-room-hall door. She frowned and leaned away; she glanced back toward the dressing room, looked through the peephole again and said, loudly, "Damn."

Grayleen poked her head around the jamb. "Now what?"

Helly pointed at the glass, then said, "The hell with it," and shoved open the door. "Look," she said, pointing. "Go ahead. Look."

"Jesus, Helly," Grayleen said nervously. "If Charity catches you—"

"Jesus H," Helly muttered, grabbed the other woman's arm, and dragged her to the door. "Look!"

Grayleen did.

Wilford leaned back against the bar, arms folded, scowling the way he always did; no one was behind the bar because they hadn't figured out who would go first. Tending bar sucked. The tips were lousy, they had to listen to the customers try out their best lines, and . . . the tips were lousy.

There was no one else in the room.

Never, Grayleen thought. Never in the few years she had worked here—on weekends, that is—had there never been at least one sorry man sitting at a table. Maybe a couple minutes after opening, maybe. But it was already past five, and the damn place was empty.

"They ain't coming," said Helly miserably.

Wilford looked over at them, scowling.

Grayleen smiled sweetly, sighed, and swallowed hard when she saw the shotgun at his side.

Sheriff Nathan's fingers fumbled the cartridges into his revolver, nearly didn't get it into its holster. By the time he loaded the shotguns, however, he figured his nerves were about as steady as they were going to get tonight. As steady as they ever got at times like this.

The others had already left, every man on the force and at least two dozen hunters who had shown up ready to volunteer. He figured twice that many were already in the hills.

His orders were simple:

If you see Maggie Medford, don't hurt her, but don't let her get away.

If you see anything else, kill it.

Dewey wanted a cigarette bad; he wanted a drink worse.

He was soaked, sodden, and shivering so bad he thought his bones would crack.

Out in the clearing, the rain fell steadily, blurring everything on the other side into dark shimmering shapes that sometimes looked like trees and bushes, sometimes looked like something looking back at him.

He kept his gaze moving, always just this side of the perimeter, so vision wouldn't play tricks and tell him things that weren't so; he turned his head by slow degrees, listening through the rain hitting the leaves; he lifted his feet carefully, one at a time, one inch off the ground, just to keep his legs working.

Watching, always listening.

Until something touched his shoulder.

TWENTY-FIVE

The stench of blood was nearly overwhelming.

Proctor holstered his gun and slapped the wall switch before he went in. The light was feeble, but enough to see more clearly the figure spread-eagled on the bed.

Blood stained the walls in streaks and blotches, darkened the bare floor as it dried into the grain. As he made his way over, he saw drops on the TV screen, across the remains of a splintered table, on a chair with back and seat, its legs scattered around the room.

And the flies.

Not as many as there would have been had the weather been warmer, but enough for a soft droning in the bathroom, whose door hung by one hinge.

He stood at the foot of the bed and looked at her.

A thin blanket lay across her middle, just covering her breasts, barely reaching her hips. Her legs and shoulders were bare and, as far as he could tell, unmarked. Wide leather straps bound her wrists and ankles to the bedposts; there were no padlocks or buckles, the straps were clumsily but effectively tied.

There was a long cut along her left cheek eye to mouth. Her lips were dark and swollen.

When she opened her eyes suddenly, he almost yelled and jumped away.

She smiled tentatively and said, "Kinky, huh?"

And cried. Without a sound. Great gulping sobs that wouldn't quit as he worked quickly, impatiently, to undo the straps at her right wrist, nodding when Taz finally joined him to work on the other side, his lips tight and his throat constantly working.

"Are you all right?" Proctor asked repeatedly.

No words; only sobs.

"Are you all right, Flower? Did they hurt you?"

Gently. Quietly. Wincing each time her sobs hitched whenever he rubbed the stiff leather too harshly over her badly chafed skin. But he couldn't help it, and he told her that too, and told her to hang on, she'd be out in a second.

As soon as her right arm was free, he paused.

And she slapped him. "God *damn* you, Proctor," she yelled, and wept again.

"Hold still," he whispered, working now at her ankle. "I don't want to hurt you. Hold still, Flower, work with me, hold still."

The blanket slid down, and he smiled to himself when he saw the effort Taz made not to look.

She was naked beneath the worn cloth, but he could see no major wounds, just a number of small scratches, a few larger ones marked by crusted blood.

He and Taz finished at the same time.

Proctor took her by the forearm and helped her to sit up, then wrapped the blanket around her, crooked an arm under her knees and lifted her against his chest.

She opened her mouth, and he told her, "Hush."

On the way out he asked Taz if he had any extra clothes, to fetch them and bring them to his cabin. He welcomed the rain. After being in that cabin, it felt good, cool, and he wished he could drink it to take the bitter taste from his mouth.

Inside again, he set her down on the bed and, after shedding his coat, took a small first-aid kit from his bag. He worked on the cheek first, dabbing away the dried blood, blotting the fresh with soft cotton.

"I saw it," she said dully, even though she tried a smile.

Frustrated that he didn't have a full kit with him, he did his best to fix the wound without hurting her. She didn't flinch; he figured she was in mild shock and the pain would come later. "Best I can do," he apologized when he was done. "I think you'll need stitches. There's going to be a scar."

"I saw it."

Gently he pushed her shoulder until she lay back, legs dangling over the edge of the mattress. He examined her legs, found a slice out of one heel, and went to work again.

"I saw it." Staring at the ceiling, hands clasped across her stomach.

Taz returned with a shirt and jeans, laid them on the table and stood by the door, watching, breathing heavily. It didn't last. He moved around the room, turning on all the lights.

"You pissed me off, Proctor," she said.

"I know."

"I didn't even try to find her right away, you pissed me off so much."

He nodded, not looking up, wrapping the foot in gauze and tape.

"I went to the kitchen, but she wasn't there. I wandered around a little, went into that shop and saw those glass doors. The museum? I wasn't there two seconds, I swear to God, and she come up behind me. I didn't hear her at all. She come up behind me and she says something. Scared me half to death, I probably yelled a little. She laughed and shoved me. I fell against one of those cases, and I couldn't grab good hold and fell to the floor.

"When I got up, ready to bite her eyes out, it was there, right behind her.

"I saw it, Proctor. I saw it."

Carefully he peeled the blanket away and scanned the rest of her, seeing nothing but those tiny scratches, nothing that needed attention. When he drew the blanket back over her, she smiled at him. Crying still. Just a little.

"Not exactly," she said, "what I had in mind."

"Get dressed," he told her. "Get warm. We'll be here when you get out."

She sat up, and Taz hurried to hand her his clothes. "You better be," she told them. "You better be, or you're dead."

After she limped into the bathroom and closed the door, he sagged, head low, hands feeling curiously numb. He knew Taz was watching, but he couldn't bring himself to beat his chest or draw on the hair shirt. He had acted without thinking and had nearly gotten this woman killed; they both knew it, and he was grateful the kid made no accusations.

They both glanced up when they heard a soft moan—of pain, and of seeing herself in the mirror.

"Shit," Taz said flatly.

Proctor agreed, stretched his back, and called, "Flower, did they get your purse?"

Her response was muffled, but clear enough so that Taz understood and left for her cabin. He knew what Proctor was after, and Proctor wondered if he also knew what came next.

"Come on, honey," Maggie whispered, still rocking, still smiling. "Come on, darling, don't be late. Maggie's waiting. We got things to do."

Dewey launched himself away from the tree and raced into the clearing, not stopping until he realized he was standing on his trap.

He cursed his stupidity and braced himself and held his breath. A hell of a way to die when you're trying to get rich, he thought as he closed his eyes.

He didn't fall.

He looked stupidly at his feet, and it took almost forever before he understood that someone had filled it in.

There was no trap.

There were no traps anywhere. Not anymore.

And when he turned around, he knew there was no more running either.

He saw the raindrops turn into hundred-dollar bills.

He saw his limousine with the showgirl chauffeur

and the real leather seats and Grayleen in a bikini waiting in the back that was big enough for twenty.

He saw a parade somewhere, confetti falling like snow, with him sitting on the back of some huge convertible car, waving to the thousands who kept calling his name.

He saw himself with a mustache so he didn't look like them dumb Amish anymore.

He saw the arm in the rain rise over his head.

He saw the claws.

He heard the scream.

Proctor grinned; he couldn't help it.

The shirt was a hundred sizes too large, the sleeves rolled up several times just to free her hands; the jeans were large enough to fit another person in, and she'd rolled them up from the bottom so she could walk without tripping.

"Y'all aren't as skinny as you look," she said, brushing her hands over the shirt.

Taz laughed nervously, shook his head, and laughed again.

She scowled at him without rancor and crawled onto the bed, wincing as she settled on her heels in the center of the mattress. One hand touched her injured cheek. Her eyes, no tears, were puffy and dark; her lips didn't look as bad as they had been. When Taz asked if she wanted a beer, she told him she would marry him if he brought her two.

He did; she sighed, and drank the first one halfway through before wincing again.

Proctor wanted to sit on the bed, get close, but a

step and her involuntary cringe changed his mind. He took his chair instead, and said, "Tell me."

She closed her eyes. "Won't believe me."

"Sure he will," Taz said tightly. "I will. I heard it."

She rocked a little, swayed a little, drank again, and shook her head as if settling her hair.

With a single finger Proctor stopped Taz from speaking again.

Patience.

Listen to the rain, and wait.

Listen to the rising wind, and wait.

"Tall," she said at last, eyes still closed. "Looked tall to me, anyway." Her chest rose and fell slowly. "It was all so fast, I didn't get a real good look, you know? He . . . it was like he . . ." She waggled her free hand. "I don't know, like he shook a little. No. A couple of times it was like he wasn't all there. Like a ghost or something. But he was. *She* was, too. The bitch. I tried to get away, and he hit me. Cut me. Then he's dragging me by the arm." She massaged her left shoulder. "We're in the rain, and I can't see him, but I can hear *her*, the bitch, talking to him." Her eyes opened suddenly. "She called him 'honey,' for God's sake." Her eyes closed. "Finally she tells him, it, to pick me up. I'm screaming like there's no tomorrow, which I didn't think there was, but no one's there.

"You weren't there, Proctor. You weren't there.

"Maybe I passed out, I don't know, I don't know much, but I'm on the bed and all tied up, and she says not to kill me, she's not ready yet. Then they're gone, and all I can think of is that I'm bleeding to death." She brushed her cheek again. "The stupid worst thing is, I'm lying there and I know I'm going to die and all I can think of is that I sure hope those flies don't start crawling all over me. Silly, right? I'm going to die, and all I worry about is some stupid damn flies."

The first can was empty; she opened the second and drank, but not much.

Proctor said, "What did he look like?"

"Strange," she answered without hesitation. "Like I said, I just saw bits, but . . . his face wasn't right. I thought he was wearing one of them Halloween masks, make him look like a cat or dog, I don't know which. I think he was naked, I couldn't tell. I think he had fur or lots of hair or something. I couldn't tell. Tell you the truth, I wasn't really thinking much at all except I didn't want to die."

She held the can in both hands, tightly, pressing it to her chest.

Watching as Proctor pushed himself to his feet, picked up his coat, hefted it, and put it on. He said, "No, you stay here with Flower," when Taz eagerly grabbed his leather jacket.

"Without a tank?" he said incredulously. "Are you nuts?"

Proctor pointed at the purse Taz had fetched for her. "Still have your gun?"

"Yeah."

"Know how to use it?"

"Yes."

His instructions were simple, ignoring Taz's protests and the terror on Flower's face: lock everything that can be locked, turn out all the lights, sit on the bed, and shoot anything that comes through the door that isn't me or the sheriff.

"This isn't right," said Taz angrily. "We're supposed to be together."

"We are," Proctor answered as he opened the door, let in the rain.

"Proctor," Flower said, tiny and lost in all those clothes.

He looked; he didn't smile.

"It's a trap."

He nodded. "Yes. I know."

TWENTY-SIX

Proctor stood motionlessly in front of the motel, hands in his coat pockets, not bothering to hide, paying no attention to the rain.

If she was up there in the trees, she could see him, and she was watching; if she was inside, she could see him, and she was waiting.

He hadn't wanted to leave Taz behind. He knew full well it was a classic case of let's split up so we can get knocked off one by one, but he had no real choice. Flower couldn't come with them; she was too badly hurt even though she probably didn't realize it yet. And Taz, as great as he was, had no experience. Not yet.

He didn't understand what they hunted.

He would go after the wrong prey.

do you believe in ghosts?

He walked toward the porch. Taking his time. It was neither bravado nor dare; he had to make sure he was right, because once inside there would be little time to think again.

The building seemed much smaller in the rain, and

more dull. The signs were unlit; there were no lights in the windows, dining room or gift shop. Water gushed from angled drainpipes at each corner of the porch.

In the far distance he heard the echo of gunshots; the sheriff hunting demons of his own.

He climbed the steps one at a time.

Once under the porch roof he wiped the rain from his face with the backs of his hands, tried to brush it off from his hair, from his neck. He felt the cold now. He felt the silence.

He felt the fear.

He reached for the doorknob, but didn't turn it.

Last chance, he told himself. Go back to the cabin and call the sheriff, don't explain, just ask for help; go back and get Taz and hope Flower will be all right; go back and get the others, get in the car and get the hell out before anyone got hurt. Find Nathan and bring an army.

Or stop stalling, and get it done.

do you believe in ghosts?
yes

He opened the door and went in, eased it behind him and waited for the building's warmth to absorb the excess chill. Then he took out his gun and chambered a round as quietly as he could. Everything was nearly dark. A single window in the dining room had its curtains open, which let in a haze not much better than a match; the same in the gift shop, only slightly magnified by reflections in the glass.

A single step made him freeze and wince—his

shoes were too wet, and now they made noise. Glancing left to right, he crouched and took them off, stripped off his socks as well and tossed them aside. Traction was sacrificed for the sake of not giving himself away any sooner than he had to.

As he sidled toward the registration counter, he listened, frowning his concentration, trying to banish the drumming of the rain, the drumming of his heart.

Nothing.

Not a sound.

A deep breath, and he leaned over the counter, searched the floor, and relaxed, just a little.

He was about to swing over so he could check the office too, when sharp noises froze him, then drew him to the dining-room entrance. They came from the back, from the kitchen, the sound of pots and pans and silverware being flung around the room, one at a time. A tantrum, or a signal.

Or a taunting.

All right, Maggie, what's the plan? he thought, moving sideways into the room between the first and second long tables. Checking the gift shop for a source of ambush; checking the open rafters for the same.

He couldn't see the back wall, and the greylight over his shoulder barely cast his shadow on the table.

Another pot struck a wall, bounced along the floor, and clattered again as if kicked away.

Sorry, Maggie, I'm not buying.

Another pot, this time a broken window.

He shook his head and wondered how long either of them could take it. There was no other way into the kitchen aside from the back door, no other way into this room aside from the lobby. Sooner or later one of them would have to move.

A check of the lobby, and he lowered himself until he nearly sat on his heels, using the bench to steady his descent in case he had to jump.

He waited.

The kitchen was silent.

As his vision became accustomed to what passed for light in the room, he was able to make out the swinging door's outline from a fluorescent bulb that burned on the other side. Every so often something blocked it briefly; every so often he thought the door moved.

Mild tremors from his cold and drenched clothing passed through him head to sole; he had to fight for several seconds to keep down a sneeze.

Then the kitchen door opened, swinging toward him, and he held his breath and aimed.

A shadow in the doorway, distorted by the light and dark.

They watched each other in silence until the shadow said, "Mr. Proctor, I'd like you to meet my Jack."

He heard it then, the soft rumble of a growl, just as he turned and the lobby light went out.

It stood in the arched entrance, as if moving through black fog.

Proctor didn't wait to take a good look; he backed away as fast as he could while trying to leave his crouch, using the bench to propel himself toward the sidewall.

It made no sound but a soft and constant rumbling.

When it moved, it seemed to glide.

Not yet, as Proctor's gun hand came up; not yet, take your time.

It stopped just before it moved into the window light, and stretched out an arm and spread its fingers.

Human fingers, until the claws began to grow.

And when it moved again, Proctor thought *feline* before he scrambled over the table just ahead of the sweeping claws. He landed on his feet, used the bench as a step to the second table, whirled and fired. Twice.

A flash of muzzle; a flash of teeth.

It cried out and stumbled, and Maggie screamed something from the kitchen door.

He fired again, it lunged, and as he stepped backward his left foot missed the table and came down on the bench instead. Toppling him as his left arm waved frantically for balance, as he pulled his right foot back in hopes of landing upright on the floor.

Little traction, and he continued to flail, hitting the next table's edge with the small of his back. Freezing him for a moment, snapping his vision off and on.

It stood above him, in the dark.

He fired twice more and knocked it howling off the table onto its back, then ran for the lobby where he knew he could find some light. Left foot skidding ahead of him, then behind, throwing him across a bench, the edge cracking against his shin and dancing sparks in his eyes, rolling him to his knees but not stopping. Never stopping. Until he reached the end and spun around, and fired.

Toward the kitchen.

Maggie screamed.

It echoed her as it rose unsteadily from the floor, still nothing more than a darker shadow that glided along the wall.

Proctor nodded without moving, and fired at her again.

It—Jack—threw up its arms and charged, and he emptied the gun into its chest, sprang the clip and replaced it as Jack fell again. Screaming rage while Maggie screamed pain, and he was almost too late to see her charge him out of the dark, a carving knife in her left hand, held low to catch his stomach.

He backpedaled quickly, just to give himself some room, but it wasn't fast enough, and she was on him. Slashing. Missing. Slashing again, once again, until he backhanded his gun hand at her, forcing her to spin away. Then he ran into the gift shop, and from there into the museum.

Here there was light.

He backed toward the cylinder and waited for one of them to appear.

He had a feeling it wouldn't be Jack, because its rage seemed weaker, more distant, and he knew why when she stood in the doorway and had to lean against the first display case, right arm hanging at her side. Fingers twitching.

"Maggie," he said.

She tilted her head. "That's my Jack, you know." And took a step toward him.

He could see the blood on her shoulder. "Maggie, Jack is dead."

"Well, of course he is," she said, tilting her head the other way. "You think I don't know that? You think this poor little widow lady don't know when she's a widow?"

Another step, and he waved the gun side to side to be sure she knew he still had it.

The knife was still in her hand as she leaned heavily against the case. "Now I know I told you that story. About my Jack? What he found?" She giggled. "No, I'm terribly sorry, that wasn't you, that was . . ." She licked her lips, pursed them, licked them again. "No, that was . . ."

"Delany," he said flatly. "Sloan Delany."

"Delany, poor Cory, oh, who cares?" She stumbled forward another step, sliding her knife-and-hand along the glass. "What matters is, my Jack is here, and as soon as all of you are gone, he'll be set to rights." She winced, hissed in pain. "I get strong again, I get some damn peace and quiet, he'll be fine, just fine."

A shadow rose behind her, a deep rumbling in its throat.

Maggie grinned, the light below turning her eyes into shifting empty sockets. "I love him," she said, close to pleading. "He's mine, and I love him."

Proctor aimed as the shadow darkened. "He'll never be right, Maggie. You'll never make him right, no matter how much you love him."

"Don't say that," she snapped. Swayed. Took another step. "You don't know."

"Yes, I do."

She shook her head wildly. "You can't. I know you can't because you never knew my Jack."

"He'll never be the way you want him," he said sadly.

And he shot her in the leg.

She screamed and went to one knee.

The shadow screamed. And wavered as here and there greylight replaced the black.

She pushed toward him, and he could finally see what he knew was in her eyes. "You'll have to kill me," she said, lips tight and drawn away from her teeth.

The shadow lurched into the room.

"Maybe," Proctor said, and aimed.

And fired again.

TWENTY-SEVEN

The cabin was much too warm, but Proctor didn't mind. He sat in his chair in clean, dry clothes, a bath towel around his neck because he couldn't stop drying his hands and neck.

Flower sat cross-legged on the bed, in her own clothes at last and winking at Taz, who couldn't stop himself from staring. Her cheek bulged with tape-and-gauze after returning from the hospital to have the injury stitched, and she looked, she claimed, like a bad boxer after a bad day. And she felt like it, too.

Taz was in the other chair, obviously trying to decide how angry, or disappointed, or relieved he should be that he hadn't been an active part of the final clash in the motel.

Proctor wouldn't help him.

He was tired, extremely tired. His back ached, his shin still stung where he'd barked it on the bench, and he kept glancing at his biceps where Jack's claws had nearly gouged him.

"I guess you won," Taz said at last.

Flower glared at him. "Young man, you stop your pouting, hear me? He was damn near killed in there, the idiot, and you could have been, too, jumping around like some kind of damn movie-star thing. Just be grateful he's a bigger jerk than you."

Proctor started to laugh, stopped himself, and shook his head.

"Besides," she added coyly, "you had to protect me."

Taz scratched through his hair, scratched the side of his neck, laced his fingers together and popped his knuckles before he held up his hands. "Okay, okay. Jeez. I just wish . . . I don't know, I just wish I had seen it, that's all."

No, Proctor thought; no, you really don't.

"Can't believe it was her," Sheriff Nathan had said as the ambulance drove Maggie away. Taz had called him during the shooting, and he'd arrived with what seemed like half the town behind him. "When I said she was a little off, I really didn't mean it like that. Grief, you know? Not crazy. I thought it just made her do some odd things now and then, that sooner or later she'd put him in her heart and get on with things." He shrugged, and had shaken Proctor's hand. "You'll have to stick around a bit, you know. Lots of questions, a statement, stuff like that."

Proctor had told him it wouldn't be a problem.

They stood on the porch, Proctor shivering in his wet clothes, even though someone had found a blanket to throw around his shoulders.

A moment later the stretcher came out, and the paramedics waited while a driver backed the ambulance to the stairs.

Proctor looked down at Maggie Medford. Her eyes

were shut, her lips moved soundlessly, and her head trembled despite the painkillers she'd been given.

"Poor little thing," Nathan said tenderly, running the side of his hand along her cheek. "But she'll get good care, Mr. Proctor, you can count on it. I suspect there won't even be a trial." He grunted. "Poor thing. Blaming it on a ghost, can you beat that?" He shook his head, adjusted his hat and belt, and walked away. Into the rain.

Proctor had told him to check Cabin Number Eight. He imagined the blood they'd find there belonged to Sloan Delany. Maybe some others, but mostly it was Sloan.

He said nothing about Jack.

By the time the others had arrived, Jack was gone, Maggie too weak to hold him, too far gone in madness to remember how to bring him back, the way she'd brought him back from the dead.

Then Nathan had returned, standing at the foot of the steps, rain dripping off the brim of his hat. He wasn't happy, for a lot of reasons. "I want to get something straight."

Proctor nodded.

"You shot her in the shoulder, that was pure chance because you were shooting in the dark."

Proctor nodded.

"You shot her in the leg to keep her from coming at you with that knife, since the first shot didn't seem to have any effect and she'd cornered you in the museum."

Proctor nodded.

"So tell me again why you shot her in the other leg?"

Proctor stared at him. "It happened so fast, those last two, that I really didn't have time to think. Like you said, Sheriff, she's a strong woman."

"Not anymore," Nathan muttered as he turned away. "Not anymore." He stopped then, and looked back over his shoulder. "Get the hell out of my town, Mr. Proctor. Soon as I'm done with you, get the goddamn hell out of my town."

Taz cleared his throat loudly, and Proctor blinked, and smiled his embarrassment for leaving them for a while.

"Okay," Taz said. "The thing is, it's over, right? Right." He looked to Flower, who nodded sharp agreement. "And it's Saturday night, right? Right. And we're not going home until God knows when the police will let us, right? Right." He rested his arms on the table, pleased with himself so far. He looked squarely at Proctor. "So what I'm saying is, boss—"

"Proctor."

"Whatever. What I'm saying is, as the junior member of this firm, and since I'm the one who came up with the connections from the library, and since I'm the one who first figured out that Delany was murdered, I figure I'm entitled to a little time off, right?"

Proctor allowed as how he couldn't argue with that.

"And since Miss Power here—"

"Oh, please, gimme a break, huh?"

"—is in no condition to go anyplace real far because of her ordeal, and since you just went through a whole lot of sh—crap, and probably aren't a hundred percent," and he held out his hand, "can I have the damn car keys so I can get out of here before I go freakin' nuts?"

Proctor didn't hesitate—he pointed to the keys on the dresser, to the door when Taz picked them up, and didn't say a word until the younger man had left. Then he turned to Flower and said, "That kid makes me feel so damn *old.*"

"Hey, you didn't undergo an ordeal, Proctor." She plucked something he couldn't see from the front of her sweater. "So now what do we do?"

"A couple of things first," he said, and reached for the phone.

"Got him."

Lana laughed, and he could hear her crying as well.

"Actually, it was a her."

"You're kidding. So when are you coming home? Doc is here too, and he's driving us all crazy."

Proctor winced at the choice of words. "Soon. We have paperwork to do, statements, and things. I doubt much will get done tomorrow, officially, because it's Sunday. Let's say Tuesday, and pray for the best."

"Okay. That'll give you time to think about this."

"What?"

"Got a call from Lieutenant MacEdan in Atlantic City."

Oh damn, he thought.

"What happened? What did she want?"

"That little weasel, Shake Waldman? Someone gunned him down the other day, smack in broad daylight, right in the middle of town."

Proctor closed his eyes and shook his head. "He called me, Lana. I should have called him back."

"You were a little busy, remember?"

"Yeah, but still . . . Do they know who did it? Was it his gambling?"

"No, I don't think so, to the first. Probably, to the second. What I know is, they found your name and number on a piece of paper in his pocket. The man who heard the shooting, a shopkeeper or something, said that he was still alive when he ran out of his store. Waldman kept saying 'Tiger's-eye,' over and over, but the guy didn't get any more, and Waldman was dead before the paramedics or cops got there."

"Tiger's-eye," Proctor repeated, and shook his head. Thinking there was something . . . he shook his head again. "I don't get it."

"It's a marble."

"I know that. But why . . . never mind. I'll deal with it when I get back."

"You do that. Now, you got a pencil? Pen? Good memory?"

Suddenly panicked, he gestured to Flower to get him something to write with, and on, and scribbled a number Lana gave him. When he asked her what it was, she told him, smugly, it was the number to call when he wanted the plane to take him home.

"Now don't take this the wrong way, Proctor," she added with a laugh, "but this is the kind of living I'm really liking getting used to."

He pushed the phone away, stretched out his legs, closed his eyes, and let himself sag until the chair barely held him.

Quiet; he loved the quiet.

And then, softly from Flower: "You were a fool, you know, doing what you did."

A sigh. "Yep."

"That friend of yours, you were too mad, you weren't thinking."

"Yeah. I know."

"That scare you?"

He opened one eye and looked at her. "Yes. Yes, it does."

"Good. Then maybe you won't do it again."

He closed the eye and smiled, let the smile drift away of its own accord, and wondered how long it would be before he fell asleep.

He might have actually dozed, he didn't know, but the next thing he knew she was kneeling beside him, a hand lightly on his arm.

"I'm hungry," she said seriously. "I am hungry, there is no pizza or Chinese or whatever you want delivery in this town, and this belle of the ball has had quite enough of these cabins for one day, if you don't mind. I want to go out."

"Taz has the car," he reminded her.

She grinned, and dangled the keys to her Mercedes in his face. "Sheriff found it on a side road while he was . . . hunting. But you, damnit, will do the driving."

When he reached for them, however, she snatched them back. "One condition."

"Agreed."

"You tell me what that crazy bitch said before they took her away."

He said nothing; he couldn't speak.

Flower told him she had rushed outside when she heard the police cars and ambulance and knew it was over, Taz complaining, but holding the umbrella to keep her dry. She saw Proctor talking with Nathan, saw Nathan leave, and saw Proctor lean over the stretcher just before they took Maggie away.

Her true age was there now. The bandage and the turmoil and the rain-dimmed light . . . her age was there, and it wasn't bad at all. She would undoubtedly have to find another line of work, but he supposed that somehow, all those texts she had read, and all those she planned to read would do right by her. Because she wouldn't allow it to be otherwise.

So why was he hesitating?

Didn't she have a right to know, after all she'd been through?

"I promise you this," he said at last, pushing a finger through her hair, "I'll tell you before I leave."

She thought about it for several seconds before she nodded, and stood, and said, "I believe you."

"Here," he said. "Take a look."

The overhead lights were on, the museum stark in too-bright light, the cases somehow smaller. Sadder.

Flower stood in the doorway, refusing to come in, telling him she could see just fine from where she was, thank you, so he stood by the cylinder, pressed it with a palm, and the front slid away to the left; it wasn't a cylinder at all. The curve and the shadows, the bubbles and the angles, he explained, made the alcove look complete. He reached in and pushed again, and the back wall slid away too, revealing a door behind it.

The thing that used to be Jack Medford could get in or out in a hurry either way. On his own, or at Maggie's direction.

"So," she said as they drove south, away from town, "you figure people are gonna think you beat me or something?"

"Probably."

"You worried?"

"Nope."

"Good. Because if you get out of line, I'm having your butt in the nearest jail."

He laughed, and knew he was absolutely right. For all she had been through, Lulu Power would be okay.

"Made him up in her head," she said thoughtfully. "Loved him so much she actually brought him back like some kind of . . . what? Ghost kind of thing, something like that?" She shook her head. "Powerful thing, someone loving you that much. I don't know if that's sick or sweet."

He didn't answer; he already knew.

"And the crazier she got, the worse he looked, huh?"

"Yeah. I guess."

And the weaker she grew, the weaker the . . . creature not quite a ghost became.

"And Cory? He knew about that thing the whole time?"

Proctor didn't think so. In fact, he supposed the sheriff really did believe it had been Maggie all along, driven mad by grief. Protecting her all this time. He supposed a strong case could be made to have the man arrested, accessory or something, but this was one of those times when he made his own call.

Nathan had lost Maggie; a prison itself.

Like Flower said, a powerful thing, loving someone that much.

He watched the road, and he wondered what something like that would be like.

"I want Chinese," she said dreamily, a few minutes later. "Lots and lots of Chinese."

"Sounds good. What about dessert?"

"If you have to ask, I'm gonna kill you where you sit."

He laughed, and she told him about a place she knew not far from the interstate overpass. The way he was driving, they would be there in no time.

"What? That far? Flower, come on, you're as tired as I am, all things considered."

"More hungry than tired. And you promised me Chinese; you owe me."

"Okay, you're right."

"And just so you don't break that promise, I got something that'll keep you going."

"If you say so."

"I say so."

"Okay. So . . . what is it?"

"I ain't wearing a bra."

TWENTY-EIGHT

Tell me, Flower said; you promised to tell me what that woman said.

Maggie lay on the stretcher, lips moving, head trembling, cold rain spilling in sheets from the eaves where the gutters had clogged. He watched the sheriff standing with Doctor Murloch, watched the ambulance pull back and an attendant swing open the rear doors.

He heard a voice and looked down, then leaned over and said, "What?"

"Jack," said Maggie, a bubble of froth glittering at the corner of her mouth.

Proctor shook his head slowly. "He's gone, Maggie. He's gone."

She coughed once, grimaced and closed her eyes tightly, groaned and coughed again.

"Jack."

"Maggie, listen, he's gone."

Her eyes opened, lashes fluttering, tongue trying to moisten her lips. "Am I dead?" she asked.

"No. No, you're not."

"Crazy?"

He didn't answer.

A grotesque smile, and he could see the faint stain of blood on her teeth. "If I'm not dead," she whispered as the stretcher moved, "then neither is my Jack."

They slid the stretcher in, the doors closed, and the ambulance left.

Proctor waited until he couldn't see it anymore, then had a brief unpleasant feeling someone was out there, watching, unconnected with the scene. Not really caring, he looked around anyway, saw no one but the cops who had stayed behind, and told himself not to worry.

Then he heard the ambulance siren.

Crying in the rain, low to high.

No, he thought, but he did it anyway—he returned to the museum before anyone could stop him.

do you believe in ghosts?

He stood in front of the cylinder and watched the bubbles rise.

Big and small.

Forever rising.

And he knew it was only suggestion when he saw the shadow inside.